The Moles

A novel by

Torben Riise

This book is a work of fiction.

Although it has its roots in actual events (which have been described in various articles over the years) and despite reasonably accurate descriptions of locations, the activities and the whereabouts of all the characters are entirely coincidental and a result of the author's imagination.

This book would not have reached its completion, and certainly not its final form, had it not been for the input of Pauline Doucette, a life-long English teacher and an avid novel reader. She proofread the manuscript and made important comments, corrections, and observations about style and content.

As always, the success in completing my books is a result of the powerful, technical foundation of the writing program I use, which was introduced to me by Brant Herbert. It continues to meet my needs even after writing nine other books. It has greatly eased the writing process and made it even more fun. I'm truly grateful for that.

These contributions have played a role in improving the flow of the story. Any shortcomings that readers may find are entirely a result of my own limitations and do not reflect upon the contributions of these individuals.

To:

Christian, Anette, and Stephen
who raised me to be the parent I am today

CHAPTER ONE

PROLOGUE

NO ONE KNEW ANYTHING ABOUT the young, aristocratic looking gentleman who recently had moved into the big mansion on the corner of Sunset Boulevard and Stone Canyon Road.

The Adamses lived half a block farther down the street from that mansion. Mrs. Adams, who wrote the Bel Air gossip column in the local newspaper, had out of uncontrollable curiosity started looking into the "new man."

She quickly learned he didn't use the the Bel Air Country Club or the adjacent golf club like almost all the wealthy people in the neighborhood, or even the tennis club. 'Well, maybe he's just not into golf or tennis,' she thought. She also knew he was away a lot. When he *was* home she observed his silver Lamborghini leaving the garage every morning heading in the direction of the beach, returning every afternoon.

One morning, Mrs. Adams decided to follow him to see where exactly he spent his time during the day. It appeared the "new man" had an office right on Ocean Drive. By spending some time around the office building, Mrs. Adams noticed he actually spent a lot of time onboard a very impressive yacht in Del Ray Marina. *Sirius,* was her name.

"Are you new to the area?" Mrs. Adams asked when the gentleman disembarked the yacht and looked out over the water as if lost in his thoughts.

"Excuse me?" he said as he turned to face the woman on the bench on the pier. He looked at Mrs. Adams, a small, lovely, mid-aged women dressed in stylish, trendy clothes, clutching a glossy magazine in her gloved hand. Her coiffure would have made Margaret Thatcher envious: Shiny white and not with a single strand out of place, even in the ocean breeze. The man decided to sit down next to her.

"I was wondering if you're new to the area," Mrs. Adams said. "I'm the owner of the antique store right down the road, and have seen your car . . ."

"Ah! Well, yes, I moved here, eh, recently," he said. "Oh, excuse my manners. My name is Nicolas d'Aubert. He pulled out a business card from the chest pocket of his navy-blue Polo-shirt, which had the name *Sirius* embroidered on the front—in cursive. He handed it to Mrs. Adams.

She pretended to look at it and read the address. Although she knew exactly which house he lived in she put on an air of utter surprise. "Oh, my! We're almost neighbors. I'm three houses farther down on Stone Canyon Road."

"Really? What a nice coincidence." He didn't add anything.

Mrs. Adams looked at the card and almost gasped. *Marquis Nicolas d'Aubert, Toulon, France* it read—in cursive. No address, though. She hesitated only for a moment.

"Um, if you would be interested in meeting some of your neighbors, I'm hosting an informal gathering on Friday evening. I would be delighted if . . . "

"Oh, that's too much. I, eh . . . "

"Not at all," she interrupted with a quick movement of her gloved hand. She rummaged through her purse and pulled out her own business card. "You don't have to answer now, but in case you decide to come, here's the address," she said and handed the card to him.

"That's awfully kind of you. I'd be glad to be there. Time?"

"Any time around 6:30-ish" was the prompt answer. Mrs. Adams got up and as she left the pier, she said over her shoulder, "Oh, and if there's a Mrs. d'Aubert, she's invited, too, of course."

"That's not the case," he answered with a smile.

#

The gathering at the Adamses was delightful. A dozen couples were there in the large Italian style mansion. All the women of the attending couples were already informed about the young marquis from France, who was unmarried, and apparently possessed considerable wealth, given his mansion, his car, his yacht, and wasn't it an impressive Rolex on his wrist? Several of the women gave Mrs. Adams a hard time teasing her about already having a crush on the nobleman, which she denied while blushing.

"So, you're from Toulon?" asked Mr. Adams while mingling before dinner. He was a tall, distinguished looking man in his 50s. His hair was still without the first silver stands, and he showed perfect teeth when he smiled. He made people relax in his presence by paying close attention to them when they spoke, and his questions reflected genuine interest. Mr. Adams was a very well-traveled man with a natural interest in places, people, and history. Put together, many thought he was a diplomate of some sort, but his background was in publishing.

"Well, I'm actually from Aix-en-Provence, a couple of hundred miles inland from the Mediterranean coast. That's where we have the family estate, but I moved to Marseilles as a young man. I didn't like the size and the hassle there, though, so I moved to Toulon."

"And when did you come to the States?"

"A few years ago."

"Wow, I could've sworn you have been here for many years, given your excellent English. American English, no less."

"Well, I was in Larnaca for several years. "

"Cyprus?"

"Yes."

"Why not Limassol? That's much larger?"

"That *was* the reason," Nicolas d'Aubert said with a smile. "Or I should say, the marina in Lanarca is much better. I was there for exactly eight years, and spoke English all the time with American ex-pats. But since more and more of my business was in the U.S. I decided to settle in California."

"What *is* your business, by the way, if I may ask?"

"Dinner is ready," Mrs. Adams said while beating an Indian gong gently.

"Oil and fuels," Nicolas d'Aubert said as they walked to the table.

It was a lovely evening.

Nicolas d'Aubert charmed everyone. His manners were "refined," Mrs. Adams thought, something that was important to her. "Did you notice how elegantly he holds his wine glass," she said to her neighbor, "three fingers on the stem. And small sips." She nodded her acknowledgement with the mind of a connoisseur. She loved friends like that.

As Nicolas d'Aubert said his goodbye four hours later and thanked Mrs. Adams with a kiss on her hand, Mr. Adams suggested a coffee meeting the following Monday. "One of my golf buddies is a salesman of fuel products; maybe the two of you could benefit from getting together." That agreed, Nicolas d'Aubert left the Adamses.

#

The meeting the following Monday gave Mr. Adams a feel for the oil business, one he knew very little about.

The golf-buddy, Ron Patterson, talked about a small company in Idaho, which he had worked for as a salesman for a couple of years. As he was more interested in learning from Nicolas d'Aubert how he had gotten into the fuel business, he quickly steered the conversation in that direction.

Nicolas explained how he as a high school student took a job driving a fuel delivery truck. "That might not sound like the most promising career," he admitted, "but I saved every penny I earned and soon launched my own trucking company, Sirius Tank Lines. From there, I leased some pumps and gradually built my own chain of filling stations, truck stops, and petroleum companies."

It was a neutral, factual outline of his business and despite his considerable success, it was void of any bragging or, as far as Mr. Adams could judge, any exaggerations. It was like a classic American success story, Mr. Adams thought.

Although nothing concrete came out of the coffee meeting, Ron Patterson and Nicolas d'Aubert agreed to stay in contact.

But something bothered Mr. Adams after they split up—something that didn't quite jibe, but he couldn't put the finger on it at the moment. He wrestled with it on the way home, and as he pulled into the driveway, it struck him.

At the dinner party, Nicolas d'Aubert had mentioned he had come to the U.S. only 'a few years ago.' How could he had worked as a truck driver in his teen years and subsequently build a sizeable company? In 'a few years,' as he had said? That would have been at least 20 years ago if Nicolas d'Aubert was in his mid-30s today.

#

In the weeks that followed, Mr. Adams pieced together what he had learned about Nicolas d'Aubert. Mr. Adams had always been curious about the stories of personalities, and in this case, he was happily supported by his "professional gossip wife," as he often called her.

His investigations were as detailed as they could be without being in France among all the nobilities of the entire Aix-en-Provence region, but much to his surprise and dismay, he did not find the d'Aubert family *anywhere*, marquis or not. He did not find any traces of Nicolas d'Aubert in Marseilles either, nor in Larnaca, Limassol, or elsewhere on Cyprus. And Mr. Adams didn't think Nicolas's excellent English suggested a French or Cypriot background.

But Mr. Adams did find plenty of stuff about Nicolas d'Aubert—with the help of another golf friend—when he turned his investigation to the U.S.. His friend was in the LAPD, and according to him, Nicolas had been investigated several times over the years—"but never convicted," his friend emphasized for the sake of good order—for selling customers watered-down gasoline, dealing in stolen fuel, evading taxes, laundering money, and assault involving one of his several bodyguards.

'Bodyguards?' Mr. Adams thought. Being a nouveau riche can attract unwanted attention, he admitted, but he had never thought of the fuel business as risky—unless you make it so. To his knowledge, none of the very wealthy families in the neighborhood had bodyguards. Why Nicolas d'Aubert?

Mrs. Adams reluctantly agreed with her husband that Nicolas d'Aubert would not be on their guest list in the future.

CHAPTER TWO

THE WHITE-HAIRED, DIE-HARD PATRIARCH, Seth Smith the Elder, husband to five wives and father of 16 children, had established a religious sect located on the banks of Tenmile River south of Boise, Idaho in 1880.

Smith was an icon in the community and the success of the sect was largely due to his visions and austere work ethics, but the lifestyle and beliefs of Smith the Elder and his followers did not meet the norms and traditions of the larger community. Although secluded and with limited contact with the Boise area community, frictions with and attempted interferences by "the Boise-folks" eventually became too much for Seth Smith, and in the early 1900, he had finally had enough.

When he decided to get away from it all, his large family and dozens of members of the Smith Order did not hesitate to follow him and establish themselves where ever he decided.

Seth Smith chose a large piece of land 50 miles north of the Utah-Idaho border outside the small village of Gooding—an ideal place away from anyone's prying eyes. It was a lush, fertile, and beautiful area with bountiful natural resources that could sustain a large Order.

Once settled with their families, the Smith Order adopted the named The Toponis Order, after Gooding's original Shoshone name, which meant "black cherries."

Over the following nine decades, the industrious, disciplined and hard working members turned the Toponis Order into a large business complex with more than 100 businesses across the North American West, including grocery stores, pawn shops, a casino, a very large cattle ranch, and a firearms company, and, collectively, they became a sizable economic base in the region.

By 1990, when Paul Smith became the number nine in the

leadership succession after Seth Smith, technology, communication, consumerism, and new norms and attitudes had transformed the country in ways that were unrecognizable from the days of Seth Smith. But those changes were not reflected in its strict, male-dominated hierarchy of the Order.

With outsiders not very welcome on the compound, family members made up much of the workforce in the Toponis businesses. All members worked hard, pooled their income and wealth, and generally lived a rigorously observant life.

Many of the workers were children. Besides helping their mothers with all the domestic chores, girls did mostly routine work like filing, answering phones in the offices, and making lunches and refreshments for the adults, while the boys worked on the ranches and in the factories.

The Order had its own school bus that would take the children to the schools in southeast Boise and afterwards drop them off at the Order's offices so they could to start working instead of going home. That was the norm; that's how they all grew up, and there were no if's or but's about it. To enforce the rigorous life of the children, strict order and corporal punishment was the norm, too. Both the boys and the girls would marry young, many of them before turning 18, and always by arrangements by the elder, male members.

But despite the strict uniformity of life in the Order, there were some outstanding exceptions.

Two girls stood out among all the girls. One was Katie.

Even as a child and all the years of growing up, she was a short, petite girl. She had short, raven-black hair and dressed more like a boy than a girl. She had sparkling eyes and a bubbly personality that often provoked frowns on the faces of the adults. She sensed that being happy was not an acceptable disposition and she felt a disconnect with the Order. Early on, Katie also displayed a keen intellect and an independent mind. The latter was generally not tolerated but being the daughter of leader number eight, Lonnie Smith and his fifth wife Helen, she had some privileges, and no one challenged the exceptions that were made in her case.

Katie was put to work in the Order's central financial office when she was just six years old. It was hard for any adult to get her to do her job and she would often be absent. When she was not around, she could eventually be found somewhere on the compound sitting in a corner, reading. At 13, she was a top student consumed by the idea of studying physics, math, or biology.

Trouble was brewing and eyebrows and voices were raised when the gorgeous, vivacious teen made it very clear to her parents that she did *not* want to marry. Ever! The discussion about whom Katie should soon marry had already come up at meetings among the elders. There were many suitors for a daughter of a leader, but after numerous attempts to convince Katie about her duty to the Order, it was reluctantly accepted that a marriage would never end well.

The other girl that stood out was Hannah.

She had grown from being the anonymous, somewhat introvert, and hardworking little kid to a model-like beauty, almost six feet tall, with delicate features and blond hair cascading down over her shoulders. Unlike Katie, she subordinated herself to the work, the routines, and the culture of the Order. It wasn't that she did not have her own opinions, but she had learned to keep them to herself. She was great at knitting, crocheting, sewing, making quilts for just about everyone, and making lots of clothing repairs for children and adults alike.

Hannah was also an avid reader and an ambitious writer. She wrote poetry, essays, and short stories, but no one ever read them since that kind of writing was considered "not Orderly." Nonetheless, she kept writing and hoping that some day she might be able to pursue a career in 'literature.'

When the right husband was ready, every one agreed that Hannah was the perfect wife, meaning that she could be relied upon for bringing many kids into the Order.

Above all the children, Matthew stood out in many respects. He was one of 39 children his dad had with 8 wives. He lived in a two-bedroom house with six younger siblings. The heating in the house rarely worked, neither did the running water. But Matthew could fix all that and more.

Matthew was also the perennial troublemaker, mischievous and often arrogant towards people who were "different." As a teenager, he did stupid, childish stuff, like small-scale vandalizing, skipping school, cutting the pony tails of the younger girls, and even spray-painting his aunt's cat. That kind of behavior would typically not be tolerated, but Matthew was extraordinarily bright and charming, and got away with almost everything.

Despite his more than relaxed attitude about school, he was a consistant top achiever at every grade level.

During the summers, Matthew worked on his father's cattle ranch in northern Idaho. That's where he learned about machines and developed a passion for engineering. By the time he was a teen, he was a tall, strong, and well built young man. Although no one would call him handsome, he had smiling, brown eyes and pleasant features framed nicely by dark, brown hair in the style of the Order: Short cut.

By the time Matthew was 17, he'd moved out of his mom's house and married Hannah, also 17.

Two years later, Matthew married 15 year old Julianna. She was one of a growing number of girls who, like Katie, resented the idea of getting married. But she eventually gave in to the pressure and married Matthew. After 10 years of misery, and without a word to anyone, she left Matthew—and the Order—by literally walking out. No one heard from her since the day she left.

In the process of accommodating marriage and her domestic duties, taking care of the children, and supporting the Order in any required way, Hannah developed a bond with the much younger Katie. It started out as a mentor-student relationship but quickly developed into a close personal bond that became Hannah's personal and mental oasis.

That caused friction with Matthew who did not have high regards for Katie, but Hannah dug her heels in. She admired Katie's independent mind and tried to convince herself—for the sake of keeping some self-respect—that she would have been equally independent and strong if she had been the same age as Katie.

"I don't understand what you get out of spending time with a girl ten years younger than you," Matthew said, trying to insert a wedge into their relationship.

"She's not a girl!" Hannah said firmly. "In this environment, she could have been a married woman with as many kids as I have. Except . . . she isn't."

Matthew huffed and puffed. "Well, I think she's putting strange thoughts into your head."

"We work well together, that's all. In between, we talk about books and science and . . ."

"And what do you know about science?" There was a trace sarcasm in Matthew's voice.

"Nothing," Hannah said honestly and without hesitation. "That's exactly why I like to talk with her. I didn't learn that in school. Katie knows . . ."

"I'd rather . . ."

"I don't need your advice on how I spend my time, as long as dinner is ready and the house is . . ." She was going to say 'clean' but changed her mind and said, "as clean as it can get."

Matthew tried to ease the tension by making advances towards Hannah, but she was not in the mood for intimacy.

Despite the not-so-idyllic home life, Matthew kept an even keel and was a steady student. He went on to earn a master's degree in mechanical engineering and a bachelor's degree in chemistry from the University of Idaho.

By the time he graduated in 2006, he and Hannah had five children. Contraception was a no-no in the Order because having lots of kids was the desired outcome of marriage. It was a lot of mouths for anyone to feed and in particular for someone who had just finished school.

But Matthew knew how to handle that, too.

CHAPTER THREE

WHILE AT THE UNIVERSITY, MATTHEW heard about a small but fast-growing industry that sounded like a great opportunity: Biodiesel.

Matthew was hooked on the idea of applying his engineering skills to a real life project, so he decided to borrow the necessary amount of money and establish a plant. Within a year, he had built a small biodiesel production plant on a piece of land his father owned near the Toponis Order.

With Hannah's help, he launched a company they called Gooding Bioenergy. They were doing well, and soon Mathew put his mother, Rita, on the payroll. She in turn soon asked Matthew to hire his younger brother Isaiah as well; he'd been out of work for some time after being sick, and he needed a job to support himself.

Isaiah was almost as tall as his brother, and with fine-lined features, thin lips, and arched eyebrows, he had a slightly nerdy appearance. Circular glasses a-la John Lennon resting on his long, narrow nose and gave him an owlish, yet mild expression. He was an active and skillful outdoorsman, intimately knowing the forests and their wildlife. He spent as much time in the wilderness as he could when he was not studying or working.

Isaiah was a mild mannered, easy-going counter-balance to the visionary and energetic Matthew. Isaiah was a master with numbers and had a keen attention to details. He had gotten a bachelor's degree in economics, so Matthew put him in the accounting office, paying him $11 an hour. He made it clear to Isaiah that, brother or not, he could be fired if he screwed up. That didn't concern Isaiah one bit. He was grateful for the opportunity and couldn't imagine he would ever screw up.

The family team was off to a good start, and even Hannah enjoyed having new activities. Gooding Bioenergy was the beginning of Matthew's rise in the Toponis Order.

"So, explain to me, why this bio-thing is so great," Isaiah asked, when he and Matthew discussed how to grow, if and when to expand, and how much to invest.

"It's bio*fuel*," Matthew corrected.

"Yes, biofuel. It sounds to me like we're just using a lot of the biomass on Dad's land, process it, and sell the final product to . . . to whom actually?"

"OK," Matthew said patiently. He had been through this in his mind many times. "Let's start with the oil crisis in the 70s, OK? You know it was caused by the embargo by OPEC, the oil producing countries, right?" Isaiah nodded. "Well, that was a serious wake-up call for the Western world. We had relied extensively on foreign countries—often unfriendly countries, mind you—to producing one of our most crucial resources. We didn't want to be in that situation in the future.

"So, the market therefore turned to alternative fuels. By the 80s, research had made great progress on biofuels made from vegetable oils, even straw and other agri products—actually, the German engineer who developed the diesel engine knew that already 100 years ago.

"As long as regular oil was dirt cheap and abundant, there was no need for biofuels. But like I said, *that* changed in the 70s and 80s. And the beauty of it all is, number one: Biofuels can be used to power trucks and heavy equipment, and used even as heating oil. Number two: It can be made from domestic feedstocks like soybeans, corn, palm, and canola, or even nasty cooking grease like the stinky stuff left over in a McDonald's fryers at the end of the day."

"I get it," Isaiah said with a smile. "But what do *we* actually do?"

"Well . . . eh, this is a bit technical. That's why I took a chemistry degree besides my engineering degree when I was at the university. Ready?"

Isaiah nodded again.

"Good. All those agri products I mentioned contain high levels of what's called triglycerides. To make biofuel, you mix one of those feedstocks with methanol, throw in a little hydroxide to start the process, which then separates the triglycerides into biofuel and a byproduct."

Isaiah reflected on this. It sounded simple enough. Then he asked, "And who buys that stuff?"

"The oil industry, those who sell fuel to their users."

"So, why sell two types of fuel?"

"They don't! They mix the biofuel with a small amount of regular fuel, typically clear diesel. They stretch it, so to speak, that's . . . "

"That's how we have less need for *regular* fuel?"

"You got it, little brother."

"And you think that's supposed to be a big business?"

"Heck, yeah!" Matthew exclaimed. "American biodiesel production shot up from around hundred million gallons five-six years ago to close to a billion gallons last year. Remember, besides the dependency issue, there was also the issues of reducing carbon emissions, and, not to forget, farmers eager for a new market for their waste products. Everyone wins with biofuels."

"Holy Toledo. Yes, that *is* a lot of biofuel. Gigantic, from my perspective. But . . . doesn't that also mean there are lots of other plants out there. Why does anyone need us?"

"We'll do it cheaper and better," Matthew stated with convincing confidence.

#

Despite the potential for biofuels, the business was terrible throughout 2007 despite the fact the Gooding Bioenergy plant was running well. Isaiah was troubled and called a meeting with Matthew and Hannah as well as their mom, Rita.

"I guess we've underestimated the logistics of the business," Matthew explained. "We're simply too far away from some of the good sources of the raw materials we need, and we buy it in too small quantities."

"Ah, so that's why we have all these bills for hauling in soybean oil from the Wisconsin and Illinois and cooking oil from restaurants and hotels in Las Vegas," Isaiah said. "I was wondering why we're doing business with all those guys."

"What's the situation with the EPA subsidies?" Rita asked.

"Let me explain that," Matthew said. "Because B100 is expensive to produce, Congress and even some states have offered up billions of dollars worth of subsidies to spur biodiesel production.

"Every gallon of biofuel made from feedstock is given a so-called RI-number, a 'renewable identification number,' by the Environmental Protection Agency, just like we know it from the carbon credits EPA issues to corporations for reducing polluting emissions.

"Two things are important here: The big oil companies are required to either buy or produce their own biofuels. But, they can . . ."

"I understand all that," Rita said, "so why doesn't that help us? Don't we get them? The subsidies, I mean?"

"Sure," Isaiah answered, "but they barely cover production costs."

"Oh! So, we have zero profit. We're working for nothing?" Rita said, deflated.

"For right now, yes," Matthew interjected in order to sound optimistic. "We'll find ways to get around it. The market is there, our plant is excellent, we run at decent capacity. There's gotta be a solution." Matthew got up.

He was hiding his own concern.

#

Matthew started looking around, talking to other folks in the industry, thought at length about Isaiah's question about the federal subsidies. Matthew had always had his ears tuned in on the conversations of the elders in the Order, and he knew the Smiths were no strangers to the idea of ripping off government programs.

He had overheard several comments that the Order recently had been forced to pay a settlement for alleged welfare fraud by having multiple wives of one husband declare themselves single mothers, destitute, and in need of state aid for themselves and their children.

Rumors also had it that the Order shuffled money around between their various businesses to avoid paying taxes. Publicly, though, there was never enough evidence to bring a case against the Order. Leader Paul Smith issued a statement that the Order "strongly condemns fraudulent business practices and stresses to members and non-members alike that this behavior is not in line with our beliefs or principles."

The matter went away.

But an idea was planted in the mind of Matthew.

CHAPTER FOUR

MATTHEW CALLED DAN HANCOCK IN Atlanta. Dan was a 32 year old, former actor with a quick mind, bedroom eyes, and a lazy smile. When his short acting career ended, Dan had gone into buying, selling, and transporting used cooking oil and other liquid fuels. He was a quick learner and had been one of Matthew's best customers. But he had one problem: He didn't produce biofuels himself. So, when Matthew suggested they formed a partnership, Dan was more than happy. It meant that Dan would have some control over all the steps of a fuel transaction.

"It's time for a meeting," Dan said. Matthew agreed.

He knew he needed to get closer to the downline sales activities himself, and Hancock offered such an opportunity. They decided to meet somewhere midway between them and chose Kansas City.

Two days later, over lunch in the airport, Dan explained how he had been able to be so successful in the past few years.

"We obviously don't need to talk about production, so let me talk about how IRS and EPA are giving out credits to companies like Gooding Bioenergy for making biofuel for B99." Matthew nodded his agreement.

"All right, so, IRS and EPA credits are earned at two different levels of the manufacturing chain. The first is the production. Every gallon of B100 a producer makes earns a 'renewable identification number,' pretty much the same way as . . ."

Matthew held up his hand in an arresting motion. "I also know that part; what's the other level?"

"OK, good," lazy-smile said. "The other level is blending. Since pure B100 is a high-viscosity product, it can be used only as fuel for trucks and heavy equipment. B99 can be used more broadly. Now, every gallon of B99 produced earns them a $1 'tax credit'—Dan fingered a quotation mark in the air—which is actually a direct cash payment from the IRS that you get when your production papers are submitted to them. The B99 then gets sold down the line to customers like fuel stations or trucking companies."

"And what's the big deal about that?" Matthew wondered. "I mean, does that work?"

"Oh, absolutely.!"

"Give me an example of how it has worked for you. I assume you have tried it out?"

"Sure. It's kind of a trade secret, except it's not, if you know what I mean? Everyone does it. Early on, before I started doing business with you guys, I bought a quarter of million dollars worth of B99 from a Florida biodiesel company, or about hundred thousand gallons. Let's call them BioABC.

"Then I, eh, shall we say fiddled a little with the paperwork to make the B99 look like it was raw *feedstock*, and then fiddled a little with some more paperwork to make it look like BioABC had processed that feedstock into B99. And then I sold the *original* B99 to one of my customers who needed it."

Matthew turned that scenario around in his head. He knew there had to be more to the story than that. "And?" he asked.

"And . . . low and behold: BioABC cashed in roughly hundred grands in tax credits! And we split it fifty/fifty." Dan sat back and watched a light go off in Mathew's mind.

"So, you made a profit on buying and selling the B99 and you made an additional fifty grand from just submitting production paperwork alone? Without producing anything?" Dan nodded. "Holy smokes!" Matthew said.

Dan and Matthew finished their luncheon and decided to look at more deals together of the type Dan had just described. Matthew could barely wait to get home and share with Isaiah how they could solve their financial problems.

#

Isaiah could tell Matthew was already applying Dan's model to Gooding Bioenergy. Knowing the production capacity of Gooding Bioenergy, he could see how millions of dollars could be made in the company. He didn't say so, but he was not happy about the fact that

Matthew was happy. Still, he was raised to believe that you don't argue with an elder brother, and he admitted to himself they needed the money.

Through 2008, business was on an upswing. Matthew, having invested in more and larger trucks, was able to buy raw material in much larger quantities than before and thereby cut the cost of bringing it from the suppliers to their plant. At the same time, customers were hot and orders kept coming in. 'They may be small,' he thought, 'but there're a lot of them.' Matthew had the plant run in 2 shifts. Business was humming.

One day, a particularly big B100 purchase request came from a company in India. It wanted more than 700,000 gallons of B99 within two weeks. That would require close to 650,000 gallons B100 before blending.

"Can we supply that much in that amount of time?" Matthew asked the plant manager.

"If we go to three shift, day and night production, yes, we can certainly do that." He looked at Matthew who interpreted the look correctly.

"Yes," Matthew said, "there will be a compensation for that."

"Let's do it," the plant manager said and nodded, energized and optimistic.

Matthew was happy, too. They had never had an order of that size before. 'Things are achanging,' he thought, giving mental credits to Bob Dylon.

When the 650,000 gallons B100 left the plant, the spirit was high in Gooding Bioenergy.

But that didn't last long.

#

A few weeks later, a message from India arrived on Isaiah's desk. While the fuel was still in transit to India, they buyer went out of business. They simply refused to take possession of the cargo when it would arrive. Isaiah called a meeting with Matthew and Rita.

Matthew was lost for words after Isaiah read the laconic message. He wanted to fight it.

"How? In court?" Isaiah challenged Matthew, who didn't answer. "It'll be in Indian court. It will be a lost case."

Matthew realized he was forced to ship back almost two million dollars worth of product, which most likely had gone rancid after sitting in hot shipboard containers for a couple of months before it would be back in the U.S.

"How on Earth are we going to recoup that investment?" Isaiah asked. "What kind of operator would buy about two million worth of secondhand, potentially foul fuel?"

Matthew didn't have an answer —yet.

Days of mulling over the problem ended with Matthew grasping at a last straw: Calling the sales person in Southern California, Ron Patterson. He operated in one of the largest and hottest markets in the country and might have some contacts.

"Worth a try," Isaiah and Rita agreed.

#

Matthew was in Houston when Ron Patterson returned his call.

"Patterson! How are you?" Matthew asked. He and Ron Patterson had always been on last name term. After a few words about families and other pleasantries, Matthew explained the predicament.

"I know someone who might have ideas or might help us directly. Hold on for a second," Patterson said. Matthew could hear papers being shuffled. "Yes, here it is. I met a successful, flamboyant *marquis* from France or Cyprus or somewhere in the Mediterranean area during a coffee meeting in Bel Air some time ago."

Patterson explained what little he had learned about the *marquis* and his business, which sounded like a large operation with trucking and storage of fuel, gas stations, and so on. "At the end of the meeting, we decided to stay in touch, but we really haven't."

"His name is Nicolas d'Aubert. Should I call him?"

"Absolutely. Go for it," Matthew said, hope rising. "If nothing else, the *marquis* might know someone who could be useful."

It took all of 5 minutes before a call came in from Nicolas d'Aubert. He introduced himself, referred to the call from Patterson, and went straight to the point. "I'll take it," he said.

"All of it?"

"Yup! As much as you have." The conversation ended with Nicolas asking Matthew to come to LA to discuss the matter, "pronto," he added. "Oh, and make sure you fly in to Santa Monica Airport, not LAX," Nicolas said.

Mathew booked a ticket to Santa Monica right away.

CHAPTER FIVE

MATTHEW WAS GREETED IN THE regional airport outside Santa Monica from where Nicolas made his way to a desolate, warehouse-lined street in the gritty LA suburb of Commerce. Nicolas had a *Sirius* gas station out there, with two grizzly bear statues standing guard in front. Matthew wondered if that was an omen, even more so because he noticed what looked like a couple of bodyguards loitering outside Nicolas's Escalade—almost the size of grizzlies. Matthew had never dealt with anyone who kept bodyguards around and he briefly wondered why that might be necessary.

Nicolas was a fit, heavy-set man, perhaps 5'7" high and about 190 lbs., with black hair and well-trimmed, black beard. His brown eyes scanned the environment all the time, but he didn't appear nervous. With refined manners and a silver tongue, he had an easy-going, worldly air to his persona. He dressed in a rugged Mid-western style with blue denims and a checkered shirt.

They went inside a double-wide trailer that served as Nicolas's field office, and while Nicolas put a pitcher of cold water on the table, Matthew looked around. It was a very well equipped office void of decorations that could otherwise have given it some personality. This was all about efficiency. They immediately started talking about the business at hand.

"So, what kind of paperwork and specs do you want on the product?" Matthew asked.

"Nothing! I take it as it is because I can get rid of it as it is." It surprised Matthew that Nicolas apparently wasn't troubled at all about the biodiesel's quality. Nicolas read the expression on Matthew's face correctly and added, "I move a lot of fuel. In fact, I dump everything from motor oil to yellow grease into our tanks." After some explanation about his operation, Nicolas reconfirmed that he would buy the fuel and pay Matthew as soon as it landed in Los Angeles harbor. "I'd also like to see your facility, because if you guys can supply, I already have many more orders to fill."

That was sweet music in Matthews's ears, and over a brief lunch on the way to the airport, they agreed that Nicolas would be visiting the Gooding Bioenergy plant two weeks later.

Although it had been a short visit, it lifted Matthew's spirit tremendously.

#

Isaiah and Rita were hugely relieved, too.

"What's he like, *le marquis*?" Rita asked with a smile before they even sat down. She was the Order gossiper and wanted all the colorful details.

"He's a short, stocky guy. Blank hair, a neat mustache and . . ."

"I don't care what he looks like," Rita interrupted Matthew with a smile. "What I meant was: What kind of person is he?"

"Honestly, I don't know a whole lot about him, but it appears he runs quite an operation. I mean, that office was just a field office close to an airport; he has several other offices. He has his big cars, his own airplane, at least I think so, since a private jet with the *Sirius* name was on the runway."

"Why would that make it his?" Isaiah asked.

"His gas stations and offices have the Sirius name and logo plastered all over the place. But I'll have Ron Patterson find out more before he comes to Gooding."

"Good idea. Back to business," Isaiah pressed on. "I have one concern. I can't imagine anyone buying any product worth two million dollars without preconditions," the always cautious accountant said. "He must be one heck of a risk-taker."

"Or is he scamming us?" Rita asked.

"What?" Matthew couldn't believe his ears. He faced Rita.

"Well," Rita hastened to add, "I mean, did you ask for a downpayment? Enough to make sure he doesn't change his mind but takes possession of the oil anyway."

Matthew looked like a half-drowned puppy. "No, I didn't ask for that. We agreed that he pays us immediately upon the arrival of the fuel from India."

"Easy to say," Rita mumbled.

"I'll call and request a downpayment before he comes out here," Isaiah said. "We cannot afford to do business without some protection, in particular for a deal with a first time customer."

"Agree," Rita seconded.

Matthew checked back in with Ron Patterson right after the meeting, thanking him for his assistance and ending their conversation with asking Patterson to find out "everything that's known about Nicolas d'Aubert, aka Le Marquis d'Aubert," in the Bel Air/Santa Monica area.

By the end of the week, a brief report about N d'A—that was Patterson's abbreviation—ticked in on Matthew's fax.

N d'A controls quite an empire of storage facilities, truck stops and gas stations across Southwest USA. I checked in with numerous people at the gas stations, filling stations, and one blending facility. They all refer to him by the name Sirius. 'That is his personal totem,' they said. Sirius is, of course, the leading star in Canis Major star constellation, and they all emphasized the words "leading" and "star." Nothing seems coincidental in N d'A's business.

He is known for cruising through Los Angeles in a Lamborghini, a Rolls-Royce, or an armored SUV. All silver. He adorns expensive watches. He goes nowhere without his black-clad body-guards hovering at his elbow. His main office is on Rodeo Drive and he lives in a mansion in Bel Air. Very exclusive.

He's big money.

RP

PS: I did not check tax records or police records.

CHAPTER SIX

TWO WEEKS LATER, NICOLAS JUMPED on his private jet with two of his bodyguards for a trip to Idaho.

On a frigid January day in 2009, Matthew Smith waited anxiously at the tiny Magic Valley Regional Airport outside Twin Falls, Idaho, for Nicolas d'Aubert's jet to arrive. Matthew desperately wanted to make a good impression, and being too embarrassed to pick up his guests in his humble 1995 Ford F-150 truck, he had rented a Cadillac Escalade.

Matthew was already on the way to be one of the top earners in the Toponis Order, but he wanted to do better. After all, he had three wives now and ten children to support. Partnering with a man who obviously knew something about making money was exhilarating.

The heavyset marquis from France or Cypress or wherever it was, stepped off the Cessna Citation Longitude plane with a pair of bodyguards in tow. Once they had settled into the leather seats of the spacious Escalade, Matthew drove Nicolas half an hour north along the Snake River flatlands, past the remote village of Gooding, and to the operation Nicolas had come to see.

Hannah, Rita, and other staff members turned out to greet Nicolas with a basket of Cyprus fruits and a cowboy hat. Both seemed to surprise Nicolas, but he graciously accepted the gifts.

Hannah observed Nicolas out of the corners of her eyes. She spoke only when she was asked for an opinion, which was not often. She admitted to herself that Nicolas was charming in a rustic way, and attractive in every aspect.

The visit went well. To Nicolas's eye, the biodiesel plant, a complex of processing vessels, storage tanks, prefab buildings, and trucks all looked modern, well organized, and well maintained. After touring the plant, Nicolas invited Matthew and Hannah to dinner.

"There aren't very many great places in Gooding," Hannah said, but that turned out not to matter.

"We're going to Seattle," Nicolas said casually.

"Seattle? What are we . . . "

"Having dinner. A friend of mine has a nice place there and I'm welcome to visit it any time."

An hour later, Matthew and Hannah found themselves aboard Nicolas's jet en route to Washington. 'Nice place' was the understatement of the year. It was a huge, Italian style mansion in three levels. The main building was at the back-end of a large garden with symmetrically designed vegetation areas, hedgerows, shady trees, and a dozens of fountains. There were statues of Roman gods and folklore legends. The ambiance was beautiful. 'In spring and summer, this place must be magnificent,' Hannah thought.

They dined on 12 small Italian specialties made right at the dinner table by an authentic-looking Italian chef. All along, a hired, local singer serenaded the group with Italian folk songs. There was no talk about business. This was all about getting to know one another.

At 2 a.m., Hannah and Matthew went off to the hotel room Nicolas had arranged for them, while Nicolas and his friends continued partying.

#

On the way to the airport the next day, Nicolas stopped off at a seafood store. "Do you like crab and lobster?" he asked. Hannah and Matthew both nodded. Nicolas bought some for himself and proceeded to buy out the store's entire stock—9 big boxes—and gave it to the host couple as a gift.

When they got back to the plant outside Gooding, Nicolas and Matthew sat down and discussed business details. The downpayment had already been paid, so Isaiah didn't feel he and Rita had to sit in on the conversation, and Hannah excused herself, too.

Nicolas talked about EPA subsidies with an openness as if they had worked together for a long time. There was nothing in the air of caution, of 'feeling one another out,' or limiting only as much information to the other as needed. This was a conversation between two partners who trusted one another. Matthew was encouraged with this level of trust from a man who clearly was successful in the business. As Nicolas talked, it dawned on Matthew that the public 'subsidy game' was far more common in the industry than he had ever imagined. Dan Hancock had already said so, and now Nicolas confirmed that.

Eventually, the conversation turned to the oil shipment from India that would soon arrive in Los Angeles. "Let's sweeten the deal with some extra credits," Nicolas suggested.

Matthew was not shy about asking how to do that, and Nicolas was more than happy to outline what they should do.

"While the B99 from India will be loaded into my storage tanks in Long Beach, the documents will declare it to be *feedstock*. Then, documents will show the newly arrived feedstock will be trucked from my storage tanks to your facility here in Idaho. Then, a third set of documents will show that Gooding Bioenergy converts it into the biodiesel it already is, and the final set of documents will show the 'newly made' B99 being trucked back down to me in Long Beach . . . where it already *is*. Voila!"

Matthew was stunned by the simplicity . . . and the audacity.

'These transactions will generate identification numbers and tax credits of more than seven hundred thousand dollars,' he thought— 'and we will not touch or move the fuel at all.'

At the end of the day, Matthew drove his new business partner to the Magic Valley Regional Airport where the Cessna jet took off and disappeared in the glowing, frosty evening sky. Matthew shook his head. 'We went from potentially losing oil worth two million dollars to gaining a profit on the sales of the B99 to Nicolas *and* get seven hundred grands in additional profit!'

When Matthew came home from the airport, he and Hannah discussed what they had experienced in the past two days. Much to Matthew's surprise and frustration, Hannah did not have a good first impression of Nicolas. She could easily separate the attractive man from the slick business man with way too much swagger and show-off of wealth in his manners, regardless of how refined they were.

"That doesn't make him a bad guy."

"No . . ." There was a long pause

"*Buuut* . . ." Matthew prompted, knowing Hannah had more to say about the issue.

"I think he's the archetype of a man with a Napoleon complex."

Matthew sat back with a quizzical look on his face."Meaning what?"

"He's short. He has to look up to see you eye to eye, even to see me eye-to-eye. Actually, he has to look up to see most people in their eyes.

Being a macho guy and being short made him feel inferior since he was a child—like Napoleon—and he compensates for that as an adult with excessive swagger, with constantly having to impress people, with cars, watches, private jet, with partying, with buying tons of lobsters and crabs to people he met just the day before, with.. . . "

"What? Hold it! Hold it!" Matthew was about to lose his temper. He leaned towards Hannah. "He's rich, OK? He can afford all of it, OK? His lifestyle looks mightily appealing, OK? Why not enjoy it?"

"All true. But things like that change a person."

"Do you know what he was like, say five-ten years ago? How can you tell if all that has changed him?"

"Right, I can't, but you cannot tell if it hasn't. And if he *hasn't* changed, it may even be more concerning. From Patterson's report, it is clear that he puts himself on a pedestal, and . . ."

"Still," Matthew tried to build a defence.

"Let's drop it. He's not my cup of tea, but that doesn't matter since I'm not the one who's going to do business with him. I would just suggest that you watch out for yourself." Matthew stared at Hannah. "Because he won't," she added.

"Yes, let's drop it. Why don't you go back to Katie and her books and sit and feel miserable while I do business with Nicolas."

"It may come as a surprise to you and you will not like to hear this, but I never feel miserable when I'm with her. In fact, some of the best time I have between days and weeks and months is when I'm together with her. "

Matthew sulked.

CHAPTER SEVEN

MATTHEW WAS PAYING CLOSE ATTENTION to what was happening in the industry. He sat in the office reading an industry article about government credits:

Bilking the governement

It is estimated that in just the last a few years, operators in the biofuel industry across the country have been charged with frauding the government out of millions of dollars in biodiesel-related transactions by submitting counterfeit RI numbers.

With all the government money available for credits, the biodiesel business is an enticing target for many players in, or not even in, the industry. Over a dozen operators have been imprisoned - including one who 'sold' $5 million worth of product without producing a single gallon of fuel.

Matthew sat pensively, rubbing his chin. The article made it evident how utterly important it is to have legitimate paper work—like dates, quantities, qualities, shipping details, incl. locations, carriers, etc., and that all these data have to be consistent between all the different sets of documents that each deal requires. 'Thank goodness for a person like Easiah with his knack for details and accuracy,' he thought, and then called a meeting with Isaiah and young Katie, who now worked directly for Isaiah because of her excellent skills with numbers.

"Because IRS and EPA are scrutinizing companies like ours, we need the highest level of quality in our paperwork. Mistakes can be costly." He didn't mention with one word that the data going into these documents might not reflect reality. Both Esaiah and Katie agreed.

Like many other companies, Gooding Bioenergy was audited by IRS and EPA in September of 2009. In the week leading up to the audit,

Matthew was nervous, but despite a day-long audit, the company passed with flying colors. Matthew applauded Isaiah and Katie for getting an A+ report on their great work.

The result of that inspection boosted Matthew's confidence, and he was immediately ready to expand his activities. And it couldn't have come at a better time.

Matthew was contacted by an Italian immigrant, Emilio Ambrozo, owner of a company in Wyoming called Ambrozo Biofuels. Ambrozo had recently produced some biodiesel, but his company lacked the proper license to make it eligible to claim renewable identification numbers. Since Matthew had such a license, Ambrozo suggested they joined their efforts.

Ambrozo had plenty of deals to move around, and the pair agreed to phony up paperwork to make it look as if their two companies were connected in such a way they could claim the identification numbers. From there, Ambrozo and Matthew faked a series of deals along the lines that Nicolas had outlined to Matthew. At year's end, the two companies hauled in more than $5 million in credits on foodstock that simply didn't exist.

That kind of successful rise in the industry raised the eyebrows of a few officials. Two months after the first audit, EPA agents came back to inspect Gooding Bioenergy's facility, asking questions about production and RI-numbers. The agency wouldn't tell Matthew and Isaiah what specifically had sparked its renewed interest in Gooding Bioenergy, but it seemed like the Feds already had their eyes on Ambrozo who was, unbeknownst to Matthew, a felon already convicted of biodiesel-related tax fraud scams. Before the end of the year, Ambrozo was in jail again, and Matthew had learned another lesson.

'That was a close call,' Matthew thought as he made a mental note to always check his partners's backgrounds, thinking about Hannah's words about Nicolas.

Even with Ambrozo out of the game, Matthew kept developing the business model, disregarding concerns about inspections. With some help from one of the people in Ambrozo's network, Matthew struck up illicit deals with a handful of other biofuel outfits scattered around the country, creating paperwork to claim federal credits for biodiesel that only occasionally existed.

At one point, Nicolas and Matthew rotated barge loads of B99 in a circle from port to port in Texas and Louisiana, claiming credits on the same batch of fuel seven times. They even reprised the India operation, buying about 100 shipping containers of B99 from dealers in Florida and Texas, relabeling it as used cooking oil, and shipping it to the *east* coast of Panama. There, it was unloaded onto trucks and sent to Nicolas's facility in Santa Monica, where documents showed it was processed into the B99 it was in the first place.

"Why go through all the trouble of actually moving tons of product thousands of miles, when you can make money by just making documents showing you were doing it?" Nicolas was elated. Thinking he was invincible, he pulled Matthew into more and more elaborate and byzantine deals. Keeping up with that, the Gooding home office meticulously produced authentic looking documentation.

"EPA can come anytime they want. They won't get us," Nicolas said confidently but without explaining how.

"So, what are we going to do with all that money?" Matthew asked. "Investing?"

"Absolutely. I started with real estate in Arizona and California, but I think we should go out of the country."

"Oh yeah! Of course. You lived in the Mediterranean area at one time. Cyprus, right? So, that would be . . ."

There was a flash of uncertainty in Nicolas's eyes as if he was searching in his memory for what he might have said about that to Matthew. He went for the safe answer. "Well, eh, I know people over there who can advise us about investing in Turkey, Cyprus, Southeastern Europe, actually anywhere we may want to go."

By the end of 2011, they had spread almost $100 million around in businesses in these parts of the world.

CHAPTER EIGHT

THROUGHOUT 2011, WHEN KATIE HAD been working for Isaiah and had access to the transaction papers for all the fuel deals, she got a good insight into the business of Gooding Bioenergy. In the beginning she didn't understand much of it, but it looked impressive to her. She wanted to learn more about biofuels and asked permission to see the production plant. Isaiah agreed that it would be good for her.

The plant manager was infatuated by the petite, now 18 year old young woman, more attractive than ever with her flashy, dimpled smile and quick mind. He knew of Katie's reputation for being die-hard against getting married, but he tried his best to charm her. Katie didn't rebuff him directly but gently let him know that she hadn't changed her mind, "so it's nothing personal," she added with a smile He was nonetheless eager to spend time with Katie and answered her many questions while walking around in the production facility. Over the summer, she had learned quite a bit about the manufacturing of fuels and how the plant operated.

One day, Hannah found Katie alone in the office while Isaiah was in Boise on some banking business.

Driven by Hannah's increasing concern about how far Matthew was getting involved in a crime syndicate, and by her feeling of being isolated in her dysfunctional marriage, she associated herself even more often and deeply with Katie.

They chatted for hours, but at one point Katie fell silent. Hannah sensed there was a problem and asked her gently about it.

"It's nothing," Katie said. "It's just . . ."

'Gosh! Maybe she's pregnant?' Hannah thought. "You can tell me, Katie," Hannah said. "I'm not going to ..."

"It just strikes me . . . well, you know . . . from working with Isaiah in bookkeeping and from the many tours the plant manager has given, I've learned a good deal more about the Gooding business. You know, from the sales and economy side but also from the production side. It's been interesting, but . . ."

Hannah nodded. 'She's uncomfortable,' Hannah thought and egged her on with a gentle "Yeees?"

"It strikes me as odd that we sell a lot more biofuel than we produce," Katie blurted out. "I mean a lot, lot more."

"I know," Hannah said calmly.

"You know?" Katie sat back as if hit by lightening. "You know? But how's that possible," she asked dumbfounded.

"The paperwork doesn't always reflect the real world," Hannah answered vaguely.

"You mean . . . it's falsified?"

"Yes."

"Hannah! You knew? How can you live with that?"

"I don't have a choice."

"But you are accepting that . . ."

"No! I'm not. But like I said, I have no choice . . . unless, of course, I leave the Order."

"That's what I . . ." Katie didn't want to provoke Hannah and the conversation turned to 'having choices.' Eventually, Katie decided to talk about leaving the Order. For a second, Hannah thought the revelation about the fraudulent business was the tipping point, but Katie surprised her.

"I want to get married," Katie said with her irresistable, radiant smile and eyes that showed her excitement.

Hannah sat with her mouth open. Katie had hinted a few times about having a boyfriend, a young man her age from high school but from outside the Order. "You're the only one who knows this, so . . ."

"Don't worry," Hannah said as she tried to gather her bewildered thoughts. "But . . . get married? You never . . . "

"I know everyone here believes I'm totally against marriage. That was never the case. There just isn't anyone *here* I ever cared for— although the production manager is kinda neat. But he's over 30."

"Man, that's way too old," Hannah said. They both laughed.

"What I was going to say was that I was against being *forced* to marry someone from inside the Order *and* someone I couldn't choose myself.

"Besides, I love *this* guy. Bryan Carlson is his name, by the way.

From high school."

Hannah was devastated but she could relate to Katie's situation. Deep down she felt the same way. The dream of having the guts to take off and do what you want to do, to be with the person you want to be with had lived inside herself for a long time, suppressed, wrapped up, stowed away, but never forgotten.

"I hate to ask you this but . . . when do you plan on leaving the Order?"

"Monday night."

"Monday night? Oh my gosh! That's just . . . four days away!" Hannah was crestfallen. She sat with her hands in the lap. "How? I mean, are you just going to walk out? You've never left the compound alone."

"I'll do a Hollywood escape. Bryan will wait for me at the end of Gooding Way with a car."

"Oh, Katie, I hope it'll be a great move for you. I know it will, I should say. You deserve the best."

The two so very different women, united in mutual affection and ideas about what a good life is, got up and hugged. Hannah did not want to lose contact with Katie, so she held Katie out arm-length.

"Here's what I want to do. I'll get two burner phones with SIM cards. That way, our conversations cannot be traced to any of the phones in the compound. You will leave your current phone behind, of course. I'll have these phones on Monday. I will write my number on a sticker attached to the battery in the phone, and I'll already have your number. No one will know we stay connected. I'll leave your burner phone in the paper tray of the copier in your office. Let's not meet on Monday."

"Thanks for everything, Hannah. You're the only reason I stayed at this place for as long as I did."

They cried and kissed while hugging, and then separated.

Monday night, Katie climbed out of her bedroom window and ran across a field. Bryan was waiting at the end of Gooding Way and took her away with him.

Hannah knew why she admired this young person. 'Katie is the wiser of the two of us. Or at least the most courageous one.'

She sat in deep thought after Katie left, saddened but with a lifted spirit nonetheless.

CHAPTER NINE

ISAIAH WAS INCREASINGLY CONCERNED ABOUT the business practices of Gooding Bioenergy and decided to confront Matthew.

"What's going on?" Isaiah asked Matthew.

"Well," Matthew started, rubbing his bearded chin. "Many of those projects you, Mom, and I have done in the past couple of years were fabricated."

"Well, I figured that much. I can tell on the numbers. It's simple math. There's no way we can produce the amount of fuel that creates the kind of earning we've had last two years. Even with the RI-numbers and credits, an income of millions of dollars per month based on two dollars per gallon would require far more capacity than we have."

"But no one knows that," Matthew stated, "so why d'you ask?"

"I want to know how long we're going to continue with that. Cheating, I mean. When is it enough? We are a very profitable company now unlike in the start-up days. Besides, IRS or EPA or whomever might find out one day. They just didn't ask the right questions when they were here. Twice, no less."

Matthew didn't seem the least bit concerned. "You're right, but the point is that IRS and EPA cross-checked all our documents when they audited us, and they found everything fine. Twice, no less," he added with a chuckle.

"What if they find out somehow next time?"

"They've looked at all our records."

"It's not a matter of documents. They are consistant. But what if they bring a technical person next time who understands production? One quick look at the facility, and a competent person would know there's no way we can produce this much."

"I doubt they have such a guy."

"Maybe you're right, but maybe not. Here's my concern. People in the industry get long sentences for fraud. Like the Ambrozo guy. We don't want to put ourselves in that position. It's not just you. It's Hannah and the kids, too. And mom." He hesitated. "And me," he added.

"Well, in *our* situation we won't be caught. Nicolas has a security umbrella that will protect us."

"A security umbrella? What the heck is that? An insurance?"

Nicolas laughed. "Not insurance; something better."

"How's that possible?" Isaiah asked, pushing his Lennon-glasses up on his forehead and locking eyes with Matthew.

"Nicolas had assured me we're being kept safe from prosecution."

"We are *being kept safe* . . . that sounds like corruption. How exactly does *that* work?" Isaiah asked. The trace of accusation was detectable, but Matthew chose to ignore it.

"Nicolas has a network of police and government officials on his pay-roll."

"Or so he says."

Matthew ignored that comment, too. "I've met a bunch of them," he continued. "Nicolas and I have regular dinners with LA-area police officers. Some of them work as his bodyguards in their off-hours. He also uses a former Secret Service agent, and at least one of his people is a Homeland Security agent. And mind you, they are all paid *very well*."

"That *is* corruption! Let's hope that will work out if we need them. But what if it's just words? False promises, so to speak? Or even worse: What if they are not fool-proof? Everyone misses something. Everyone is too slow at times. Everyone makes mistakes."

Isaiah was concerned about Matthew's answers. It wasn't the first time he felt Matthew didn't look at their business in an objective manner, but now the business sounded more and more nefarious, and, on top of it, involved a clandestine umbrella.

"You worry too much, little brother," Matthew said with his signature flashy smile and got up, patting Isaiah on the shoulder.

"And you worry too little, big brother. One comment before you go," Isaiah said and waited until Matthew sat down again.

"Nicolas is running your life. When he says 'jump,' you ask 'how high?' You're starstruck. You wear the same kind of expensive shirts and shoes as Nicolas does. You both have glittery Rolex Galaxy watches. And after all these years, your beard is trimmed to look more like Nicolas's. Man, you've even let your hair grow longer. And you've changed your aftershave to the one Nicolas uses— *Brut*, if you don't remember it. *You* may not think so, but like I said, Nicolas is running your life."

That stung.

Matthew sat for a moment without saying anything, looking down and shaking his head dismissively.

Then he got up, and left Isaiah's office.

CHAPTER TEN

ISAIAH OBSERVED THAT THE MORE money they received from the US Treasury, the more ideas Nicolas had about what to do with them, and he frequently asked Isaiah to transfer money to obscure accounts outside America. Matthew flew to LA for deals and investments. Together, they traveled around the world, buying property, visited Malaysia, Venezuela, and Belize, where they invested in a casino, and Turkey, where they sank cash into a range of agricultural businesses. Hanging out with politicians, high rollers, and prime ministers in lounges, nightclubs, and ritzy hotels became the life style of Matthew when he was away from home.

Over time, Isaiah was instructed to send almost $100 million to Nicolas's connections in Turkey and Cyprus.

Toponis Order members were beginning to wonder why Matthew was suddenly living like a movie star while so many of them were struggling.

"It's part of the job. I need to project an image of success so people want to work with us."

"But . . ."

"It will benefit all of us, eventually. You all know as well as I do that Gooding Bioenergy buys goods and services from businesses owned by other members of the Toponis Order. That's how our collective businesses benefit. By my last counting, Gooding Bioenergy has steered more than twenty-five million dollars to other Toponis-related businesses."

That quieted the criticism of most —but not the concern of some.

In the process, Hannah felt she was losing her husband. One night, she decided to challenge him on the whole operation of the company.

"Let me ask you something," Hannah said one night after a long pause of reflection.

"Ahum."

"Why do you keep doing this? Making deals like this over and over again. And bigger and bigger deals?"

"What do you mean 'why'? That's what business people do."

"I know, but isn't there a time when it's enough?"

"As long as there are deals to be made, no!"

"But you guys made more than hundred million dollars last year. Why is that not enough? What more to you need? Or rather, what more do *we* need?"

"I don't know if there's an answer to that."

"But . . ." Hannah shook her head. "We can't consume more. We don't need another big car or an even bigger house. Are you happier with two-hundred million dollars in the bank than one-hundred million?"

"I don't look at it that way."

"That's what I'm trying to get at. What way *are* you looking at it? I mean, how much longer are you going to do this?"

"I haven't thought about that." Matthew was deflated. 'Clearly, Hannah is not excited about success,' he thought.

"Let me ask something else," Hannah pressed on. "You don't '*do business.*' You do some but mostly, you're defrauding the government out of hundreds of millions of dollars. It's criminal!" Hannah could not hide her dismay about that simple fact.

"Well, as long as they happily pay for these deals, I'll take the money."

"Matt! They pay for B99 to be produced and mixed. They never intended to pay for deals that have no substance to them. I mean . . . you're shuffling fabricated documents and receive huge checks based on that. Not based on sale of biofuel. Do you think that's OK?"

Matthew was shrugging his shoulders. 'He's past the moral, ethical aspect of life,' Hannah thought. Hannah was getting beyond frustrated over Matthew's callousness.

"Let me put it a different way. Doesn't it bother you that you're stealing public money, plain and simple."

"No one feels that. No one misses the money. The government already has the money."

"Would you steal from your neighbor? Or shoplift?"

"Of course not! What kind of question is that?"

"A very simple one. So, why wouldn't you?"

"That's taking money from a person, an owner, an individual. I would never steal a penny . . ."

"I'm not a national economist," Hannah said, cutting Matthew off, "but I know enough to know that the government doesn't have it's *own* money. They don't produce or sell anything. The government has *our* money, the money of our neighbors, of the shopowner whom you respect; the individual that you wouldn't steal a penny from—monies collected through taxes and what not. If you get hundred million dollars from the government, that is about one dollar per household in this country—*every time* you make such a deal. That money is flowing from *their* pockets, *through* the Treasury, and into *your* coffer. That's the issue here."

Hannah looked at Matthew, hoping there would be some kind of response or visible reaction, but there was none. Rather, there was a bored expression on his face. In a way, that concerned her even more. She reflected on her life with Matthew as she had done many times recently.

He was never home, he did not fulfill his role as a father with growing children, and he clearly preferred to stay with his other wives than with her, and their conversations had frequently became testy discussions. Hannah's only real friend was Katie. And that was now a relationship by phone.

"I do not want to be an official part of this business. I'll ask Isaiah to take me off of all corporate papers that were made when we started Gooding Bioenergy—and file amended ones. It won't change anything, practically speaking, but that's how I want it."

Matthew shrugged his shoulders again, realizing Hannah had become withdrawn in their relationship. He had even confided to Nicolas that Hannah was unhappy with him being away from home so much. Nicolas had the same solution to this problem as to any other problem: To solve it with money. "You need to buy a really nice house. That'll make her happy."

"But we already *have* a nice house."

"A nicer one. Closer to the office in Gooding and near the river."

A few days later, Matthew toured a coffee-colored, 6 bedroom, $3 million mansion near the city.

"That's it," Nicolas said when Matthew shared photos of the house. "Just your style."

Matthew bought the house the same afternoon.

When Isaiah, now the CFO of the company with a nice $300 grand house, learned about Matthew's purchase, he felt a pang of . . . not exactly envy but a bit of betrayal, perhaps? Being single, it wasn't that Isaiah needed or wanted a whole lot, and certainly not a larger house or more possessions. As an outdoors man, he could live in a small, simple, even primitive abode. Impressive houses . . . didn't impress him.

Still, it struck him that Matthew considered his own welfare and luxury before anyone else's. 'But mostly,' he said to himself, 'we are no longer the four equal partners we set out to be after the successful start-up.

He concluded he did not want to be *as active* a partner in the future as he had been in the past couple of years.

CHAPTER ELEVEN

SOMEHOW NICOLAS SENSED THE FEDS were getting closer.

"What's going on, Matthew?" Nicolas asked after a business meeting in Los Angeles.

"With what? Business is better than . . ."

"Not that. Something is leaking. Or rather, someone is talking."

"Why do you say that?" Matthew had no idea what Nicolas was referring to, but he knew people in Nicolas's operations were having antennas up all the time.

"I have this feeling that the government is looking over our shoulders. More often and closer than before," Nicolas said without giving any specifics.

"Is that a problem? I mean, they have already audited us three times and they found everything fine. Every time. So, what's . . ."

"We need to keep a close eye on all our connections, starting now."

"I agree. You are the one with the most people in your operation. Shouldn't we . . .?"

"Yes, we should. And we're starting in Houston tomorrow."

On a nice spring morning in 2012, Matthew flew to Santa Monica and went to Houston with Nicolas on his private plane. They were, among several things, meeting Dan Hancock from Atlanta, who had collaborated with Matthew at all levels of the business for a couple of years and had a fair amount of inside information about the Sirius-Gooding Biofuel business.

During lunch, Nicolas—out of earshot of the waiter and other guests—suddenly said, "Dan! Do you care about what this man has done for you?"

"Of course," said Hancock. 'What kind of questions is that?' Hancock wondered, his lazy eyes showing suspicion and rising fear.

He knew Nicolas had something in mind when he asked bizarre questions. And he also knew Nicolas had a reputation for being unpredictable and eruptive.

"Would you do anything for this man?"

"I guess. Of course, that depen . . ." Hancock was looking for the meaning behind those questions when Nicolas cut him off. "Like leaving the country?"

"What d'you mean? What's the problem here?" Hancock was terrified.

"I'm worried because you're weak. If they come at you, you'll talk."

"Who are 'they'?"

"You should know that, damn it. I shouldn't have to tell you. Let me just say this: Somebody's talking. I don't know if it's you, if it's your wife, or who. But somebody who knows a lot about the transactions we do in this operation—and you're one such guy— is talking."

#

Despite this atmosphere of uncertainty, Nicolas and Matthew kept chasing more and bigger deals. In April 2013 alone, Gooding Bioenergy banked $75 million in IRS tax credits, but Nicolas still wanted them to up the ante and nothing seemed to get in their way of doing it. By the end of the year, Gooding Bioenergy had filed for and received credits totaling $350 millions. At that point, the company wasn't producing any more biofuel than a few years after they started the business.

Isaiah kept tabs on the monthly sales, so he knew where they were heading. Still, when he added up the numbers for the year, he freaked out.

"What the Hell are you doing?" he asked Matthew. "We are getting close to half a billion dollars out of this puny little company in Idaho. You've sentenced all of us to a long, long time in prison!"

"Isaiah, you need to relax."

"Matt, we officially sell twenty-five times more biofuel from a plant that has only doubled in capacity since we started. *Anyone* can see something is wrong."

"There's nothing to worry about," Matthew said as calmly as he could. "Remember the umbrella? Nicolas has all that under control."

But in early February of 2014, the sky was getting darker. Isaiah got a call from a Mr. Michaels at the Utah IRS office informing him that

Federal agents were planning to raid Gooding Bioenergy's offices.

"Are you sure it was IRS?" Matthew said.

"I only got the name John Michaels. I don't know who he is, but that's what he said."

"Well, find out, asap," Matthew snapped. "If the Feds plan a raid, they usually keep that very secret. I have four questions: One, why does IRS and not The Fed call us. Two, it is true? Three, if so, who wanted to warn us? Four, are they friendly or do they want to scare us?"

"Why don't you have Nicolas's network find out," Isaiah calmly retorted. "That kind of digging is not something I'm skilled at doing."

Matthew frowned and let it go.

The sky was indeed getting awfully dark.

Matthew called Nicolas. The conversation was intense. Matthew suggested they should question Dan Hancock again.

"He's not a problem," Nicolas said matter-of-factly.

"No? Have you already talked to him? Is he clean?"

"He will not be a problem in the future, that's all," was the terse answer. Matthew was bewildered.

"So, we can still use . . ."

"You ask too many questions, Matt. He's not in the business, OK."

Matthew did not like the tone of Nicolas's voice and in particular not the implication. Matthew knew Hancock was successful. 'Maybe too much for Nicolas's liking? Nah. No one in the industry is as successful as Nicolas. So, why would Hancock get out of the business? He's independent,' Matthew reasoned, 'Nicolas can't fire him. Was he forced out? Of course, Dan might just have wanted to stop, having had enough already, like Hannah had said about me.

'Too many unanswered questions.'

Matthew sighed and decided to brush it off.

#

With Katie no longer in the Order, Matthew asked Michelle, a 15-year old niece, to shred all Gooding Bioenergy's documents that were not needed. Although she had recently been asked "to correct some mistakes in the production computer records," Michelle had no knowledge of Gooding Bioenergy's business. She was also asked to replace the hard drives on all computers belonging to Matthew, Isaiah, and Rita "with more modern ones." Isaiah grabbed binders full of documents and stashed them in his car.

Matthew then called Nicolas.

"We did some spring cleaning in the offices, just in case," he reported.

Nicolas was pleased with that action and was, as always, undisturbed and very soothing. "I checked, by the way, and just for the sake of good order," Nicolas said with conviction. "There's *not* going to be a raid."

#

The very next day, a wintry Saturday morning at 7 o'clock, a swarm of IRS and EPA agents rousted Matthew and Hannah from bed.

The investigators had apparently gathered enough information for a search warrant. Matthew watched as they rummaged through his office and his home for a solid five hours. Meanwhile, more agents from the EPA and IRS were searching several other Toponis-related offices in Idaho.

But once again, they didn't turn up much. Federal agents complained that computers had been wiped clean or recently replaced without backups, and they found empty desks and empty bookcases with dust patterns revealing where binders recently stood.

"Modernization, upgrading, and spring cleaning," were the words Matthew, Isaiah and Michelle all used to explain the status of the accounting area. And with no one checking the physical capacity of the production plant, the agents did not find anything. "Sloppiness, perhaps, but nothing irregular." A warning about better bookkeeping in the future was politely acknowledged.

Because Nicolas's claim that a raid would not take place had been wrong, he was rattled.

Later that week, Matthew was in Las Vegas meeting with Nicolas in the Presidential Suite at the Intercontinental.

"Strip down to your underwear," Nicolas said. "My assistant here" —he nodded in the direction of one of his body guards—"will check for wires."

"What? Are you nuts? That's an insult, Nic. You would never subject yourself to that."

"Of course not. But I call the shots here. Strip down."

Fuming, Matthew complied, and when they were done, he asked with caustic sarcasm, "Happy?"

"Yes. Here's why I go through this. I had no idea the raid was coming, but . . ."

"Shouldn't you?"

"Yes, and under normal circumstances, I would. But sadly, this is not 'normal circumstances'. The leak I'm looking for must be inside your circles. So, since I *want* to make sure it cannot happen again, I take steps like this, like it or not.

"Now let's finish our business."

CHAPTER TWELVE

MATTHEW AND HANNAH SAT IN the livingroom on Valentine's Day in 2014 partly watching the TV news, partly reading magazines and books. The breaking news story was about a young man who was killed when his car blew up on the road between Idaho Falls and Jerome in the middle of the day. The man had not been identified and the police had no information about the cause of the explosion.

It was big news in such a small town and Hannah shuddered by the mere thought about tragic events like that.

The following night, the TV news reported that the victim of the car explosion was a young man named Bryan Carlson, a former student from Gooding and later a carpenter contractor in Idaho Falls. It sent shivers down the spine of Hannah and over the following days, she went into a depression. Matthew tried to understand why "that terrible accident" as he called it, affected his wife so deeply considering she didn't even know the man. But she clammed up and completely shut Matthew out of her life.

The story went across the country, and it didn't take long before Nicolas called.

"I heard through the grapevines," he said, "that the guy who blew up outside Idaho Falls was married to a woman who used to work in your offices. Can you explain what's going on?" The tone was icy. Matthew tried to contain Nicolas's temper which he knew first hand could be "explosive."

Calmly and very factually he managed to say: "I have no idea. What I know, I know from the TV. What's there for me to know about car accidents in Idaho, regardless of . . ." Matthew interrupted himself. "But you seem to know more about it than I do. So tell me what you've heard." As there was still no answer, Matthew continued, "OK then, let me just add this: I have never met or even heard of a man of that name on our compound. Actually, had it not been for the mentioning of his name in TV yesterday, I wouldn't have known it at all. On top of that, how would I know whom a total stranger is married to? It was never even mentioned on TV who his wife was."

While Matthew let the questions hang in the air, he tilted his head, rubbed his beard, squinting. "Good questions, right?" Before Nicolas could react to this barb, Matthew continued, "Let me ask you something." There was an unmistaken hint of accusation in Matthew's voice, when he continued. "Who in your network looks into the lives of citizens in a small town like Idaho Falls? And how do *you* know Carlson was married to a someone who's not even in the Order today?"

"You don't need to know any of that," Nicolas said in a sharp tone. "I look over the shoulders of everyone I do business with. Although I trust you, you are not an excep . . ."

Matthew hung up and shut the door to his office. 'What the Hell is going on?' Question after question assaulted his mind. 'What is Nicolas up to? Why is he looking over the shoulders of people with absolutely no connection to the business of Gooding Bioenergy? Or even me and Order members, for that matter? Does Nicolas have people stationed near the Order to spy on us? Most importantly, if Nicolas has the answers to those questions, why should I not know them? What is Nicolas hiding?'

Matthew wondered if he should cool down the relationship with Nicolas. 'I'm not forced to do business with him or any of his contacts.'

CHAPTER THIRTEEN

HANNAH AND KATIE STAYED CONNECTED, mostly by text messages on their burner phones and only occasionally calling one another. Katie was happy in her new life in Idaho Falls. Although it was a small place by most standards, the city was large compared to Gooding, and she felt liberated after leaving the Order. She had a job at the library in Idaho Falls which satisfied her voracious appetite for books and learning without sacrificing her dream of being a physicist of some sort. Bryan's carpenter business was going very well.

Katie was utterly content with life.

Until the day of the car explosion.

"Can we meet?" Katie asked as soon as Hannah picked up her call. It was only three days after the accident, and Hannah knew Katie needed support and had no one else to turn to.

"Of course. Any time. Where do you want to meet?"

"Idaho Falls would be ideal, eh, since I don't have a car."

"Idaho Falls it is." They decided on the place and time and hung up.

After an emotional greeting, they sat down inside the street corner coffee shop next to the library. Between wiping tears away, Katie told Hannah what had happened and what the police thought about it.

"I had the car that Friday morning, it was Valentine's Day no less, and went downtown shopping. Bryan had left early in the morning with a colleague. We met a couple of hours later because he needed the car to go an appointment in Jerome. I would just walk home. It was cold but gorgeous, and I love that walk so it was not a big deal for me to walk home. Where was I? Oh, so after putting my stuff into the car, he took off and I headed home. It was not until the police arrived at our house that . . ."

Hannah held her hand and let Katie take the time to collect herself.

"What do you think happened? Does anyone know?"

"It's all speculation at this point . . . but the police have determined the explosion was caused by a plastic explosive, not an engine failure or anything like that. So, the conclusion is that it was a deliberate act. There was a window of two-to-three hours when I was not near the car; that would be long enough to plant an explosive device under the car. The people, eh, let's call them 'the bombers,' clearly assumed I would be driving away in the car at some point in time. The device was probably programmed to explode shortly after it started driving . . . Since I was supposed to have been in the car . . ." Katie choked on the next sentence, "there's no doubt in my mind that *I* was the target, not Bryan." She covered her face.

"There're a lot of unanswered questions," Katie said when Hannah asked where everything was at the moment.

"The biggest one is, of course: *Why* was I the target? I've been through this over and over again in my mind but I see no reason why Bryan would have been the target. Oh, I'm repeating myself."

Hannah asked herself the same questions, trying to make sense of it all. She sat for a moment and then asked: "Assume all this is correct, *who* would know something about you that would make them want to kill you?"

"It *has* to do with the Order. I'm certain of that. And if not for religious reasons, I can only think of revenge for . . . No, let me rephrase that. I can only think of it as an act to silence me. And I can't see a reason to silence me over religion, or lifestyle, or anything of that nature. I was a nobody in the Order. So, it has to do with the oil transactions."

"You mean the papers I copied and had Bryan pick up and bring to you?"

"Yes."

"But that was only three-four times."

"I know, but the papers were damaging to the business. That could've been enough."

"As they were supposed to be, yes. I see. But still, *who* would know you did that?"

"I have no idea, but it's gotta be someone inside the Order, or someone from the outside who has been spying on people in the Order." She hesitated but continued after a moment. "It could be Isaiah. Or Rita."

"Or Matthew," Hannah added with a shudder.

"You said that. I didn't want to make the assumption."

"That's OK." Hannah patted Katie's hand comfortingly. "I do think it might be at least a possibility. And thinking about the three of them, if they were committed to continue with the business, they had all the reasons in the world to prevent the leak of information . . . if that's what they thought was going on." Hannah sighed.

"And there have been a number of investigations into the business," she told Katie. "Maybe Nicolas and Matthew just *guessed* or *assumed* that information must have been leaking since the company was being investigated . . . which, of course, *was* the case since Bryan contacted FBI. Does that make sense?"

Katie nodded.

"And . . . it would be a logic guess that it would be a person connected with Esaiah who has in his office all the documents that were copied and leaked." Hannah bit her underlip as the conclusion dawned on her. "That includes me," she whispered. Katie covered her mouth.

"Both of us," Katie whispered back. "So, their guessing is correct!"

"It is. But it's still only a guess on their part," Hannah added, "meaning: They don't *know* they are right! What a bizarre situation."

They both sat in silence for quite some time, wrestling with their own questions—and formulating the next, important one.

"How do we prove any of that?" they asked in unison and started to laugh.

"I guess I'm the closest one to do that," Katie said after a moment. "I'm already working with the police. I actually have a meeting tomorrow with the chief detective on the case. He has not seen the papers you copied for Bryan and me."

"Well, we have to be extremely careful," Hannah said. "We are the *only ones* who know for sure who the moles are. We are also the *only ones* who know we are in connection with each other. *That* has to stay that way! Besides that, we know we're dealing with criminals who do not shy away from deadly force—even based on pure guesswork—to protect themselves. Tomorrow, I'll get four more SIM cards with new phone numbers so we can keep swapping them with the ones in our burners. That way the phones will have no valuable on the cards if found."

"How will I get them if we don't meet?"

"Which we definitely shouldn't; we have to assume you will be shadowed everywhere," Hannah said. "I bet the police will put a tracer on you and have a bodyguard in disguise nearby you at all times. I guess you can organize with the detective. . . what's his name, by the way?"

"Patrick McInnes."

"Irish?"

"I suppose so."

"OK, let's call him, say, uhm, how about . . . Macki." Hannah frowned. "What was I saying?"

"Organize something with the detective," Katie said with a smile.

"Yes! Right. We can possibly organize that Macki gets the SIM cards to you. I can place a SIM card in a book at the library on a certain page that we'll inform him about. That way, we don't have to meet."

"You read too many spy novels, dear," Katie said laughing.

On this high note, feeling uplifted by meeting face to face and by the sense of a common goal amidst tragedy, they got up and hugged.

"Good luck tomorrow," Hannah said.

CHAPTER FOURTEEN

KATIE MET WITH POLICE DETECTIVE Patrick McInnes at the police center in Idaho Falls. He greeted her in the lobby.

'Definitely Irish,' was Katie's immediate reaction as she followed a step behind him down the hallway to his office. Besides his last name, the thick and tad long reddish-blonde hair and blue eyes were give-aways of a northern European. He was of medium height, 5'10"- 5'11" perhaps, and well built. There was energy in his strides.

While McInnes fetched coffee for both of them, Katie sat with her hands folded in the lap and looked around. The office was warmly decorated, not large but with many personal items, pictures, diplomas, and a few colorful travel posters. 'No family photos,' she noticed, nor ashtrays. 'Thank goodness,' she thought. 'The flowers in the vase to the side of the desk needed to be replaced,' she thought. 'All in all, not what she expected from a man's office . . . 'but why am I thinking about little things like that?' she wondered nervously. Her thoughts were interrupted when the detective entered again.

McInnes started out by asking Katie to call him by first name and not use any formal job title. "*Sir* would be nice, though, but that's it," he added with a chuckle.

He asked for the information Katie had collected. She pushed a large pile of documents across the desk. Patrick put them to the side without looking at them. He asked Katie to give him a brief outline of the B100 and B99 business, the IR-credits from IRS and EPA, as well as the book keeping details of Gooding Bioenergy.

"How and why were you gathering that information?" Patrick asked. "I mean, what were you going to do with it?"

"I had help from the inside with making copies of everything. Bryan picked up the information when he visited the offices for carpentry work, which, of course, was ordered by the person who made the copies." She smiled. "Bryan and I wanted to go to the FBI, I guess, or whatever federal agency would be the right one. IRS or EPA, perhaps. Because of the nature of the crime, we didn't think it was a matter for the police."

"And did you succeed?"

"Well, it took quite some time. It apparently is hard to get a meeting with the FBI, but Bryan eventually got a phone number of an FBI officer. At the officer's request, Bryan sent an email summarizing the Toponis Order, the business of Gooding Bioenergy, and references to information we had about the fraud perpetrated by Gooding Bioenergy's leaders and partners. We haven't heard anything from FBI since."

"Nothing?"

"Not a word."

"How long ago are we talking about?"

"Oh, about two months, I guess." Katie thought for a moment. "Yes. It was in December last year."

"And how damaging was the information? In your opinion." Patrick asked.

"Very." Katie went on to explain how much money was generated in these transactions, and added: "These deals were often made without producing any fuel at all. But the cash credits were collected, nonetheless."

Patrick McInnes was flabbergasted. He sat back and contemplated the magnitude of the crime.

"This is a huge case," he finally said. "My field is, of course, the murder case, and from what you just told me, I now see a clear motive for silencing you. Losing half a billion dollar in business definitely prompts reactions, sometimes fatal, unfortunately. Having a motive is always an important step in a murder case.

"But it's also a case of criminal fraud at the highest level, which I don't know much about. So, the first thing I need to do is to get agents from FBI, IRS and EPA involved. We need their assistance, and the information you gave me here is definitely important to them. I can guarantee you we'll get their attention and they will act very soon."

His eyes rested on Katie, firmly but comfortably. He was articulate and smooth in a way that built trust. Katie needed this kind of comfort and stability in her life more than ever, and she was drawn into his personality. They both sat for a moment, lost in their thoughts.

"We need to tighten the rope around all the players in your network . . . I'm sorry, I didn't mean *your network*," he added when he saw Katie's frown. "I was going to say all the players in the network inside *and* outside the Order. We don't want to exclude or overlook *anyone.*

"So, I need your help with a list of everyone who has done business with Gooding Bioenergy in the past several years - to the extent you can remember it."

Katie nodded. "I'll get that to you today."

"Excellent." He was struck by the determination in Katie's voice. "And . . ." Patrick hesitated. "I'm sorry I'll have to involve you in a number of practical issues in the coming days and weeks. I may even need you as a bait." There was no flinching in Katie's eyes when Patrick used the word 'bait.'

"I'll do anything you need me to do," Katie said firmly.

They got up and Patrick squeezed Katie gently as he put an arm around her shoulders and guided her out of the police station.

"Do you need a ride?" he asked.

"No, I'll walk. It's beautiful out there today and I like a brisk walk in this kind of weather. But thanks."

On the way to the library, Katie stopped walking and texted Hannah's burner:

> *Macki is nice. Progress.*
> *Gotta run; going to get some new books.*

Half an hour later, another mail ticked in on Hannah's burner.

> *Just got To Kill a Mockingbird - Today.*
> *I'm already on p. 169.*

There was no code for a meeting, but Hannah knew there was some information or message for her and that Katie needed her to get it *today.*

With Matthew away for a couple of days, Hannah told Isaiah she was going to the library in Idaho Falls to get some new books.

As soon as she got there, she went straight to the fiction section and started to search.

"Let's see. L. Lee. Harper Lee. Uhm" She scanned the books on the shelf. "There!" Hannah opened the book she was looking for and went to page 169. She smiled when she saw the note there. She removed it, read it, folded it, and put it in her pants pocket.

Hannah wanted to pick out another one of the Lee's bestsellers while she was there. There was only one other on the shelf. She pulled it out and looked at the cover: *"You Are Stronger Than You Think: Never Give Up.* "Hmm, how appropriate is that?" she said to herself. She inserted two SIM cards between p. 191 and 192 and put the book back on the shelf.

She browsed a little longer, picked out Hemingway's *The Sun Also Rises*, went to check out the new book for herself, and headed home. As soon as she was back, she texted Katie:

> *You will love Lee Harper's 'You Are Stronger*
> *Than You Think: Never Give Up.'*
> *Read 191 pages already.*

In the next few hours after getting back to the office where Katie used to work and where she worked by herself now, Hannah went through dozens of computer files. As per Katie's request, she compiled a list of 75 customers that Gooding Bioenergy had done direct business with in the past 3-4 years, with names of buyers in those companies, and the Gooding Bioenergy sales persons or intermediary, if any. She printed the list in a font so small that it all fit together on one half page. She tore that half off in a casual manner, so if found, it would appear as a discarded, useless document.

Early the following morning, Hannah went back to the library. She had thought about using Laura Hillenbrand's *Unbroken* for the message transfer, but it was a very popular book and could easily be checked out before Katie could get to it. Hannah chose *Seabiscuit* instead. She placed the half page of paper between page 212 and 213, put the book back on the shelf, and left.

Hannah sent a text to Katie while sitting in the library parking lot:

> *If Macki likes horses, he would love Hillenbrand's Seabiscuit.*
> *Say hi on 2.12.*

She went home with a sense of having accomplished something meaningful for the first time in . . . ages. At least she hoped so.

Later in the afternoon, a text flashed on her burner, confirming her hopes:

> *Macki got it - loves it.*
> *Also, he met SIM yesterday.*
> *He says Thnx.*

CHAPTER FIFTEEN

DETECTIVE McINNES REQUESTED A MEETING with Linda Barnes, Director of the FBI's Salt Lake City Field Office, insisting it was urgent. She immediately confirmed a meeting time.

Before Patrick left Idaho Falls, he read Linda Barnes's profile and career, of which he knew nothing. He was impressed.

After a decade in the Utah police force, Linda Barnes joined FBI and worked as an operative in many different countries. Her stellar performance earned her a series of promotions, and over the following three decades she reached the pinnacle in FBI—outside Washington DC that was, where many attempts had been made to bring her to the national head quarters. Life in Utah, however, was far more appealing to her, so she declined. Now, in her early sixties, she coordinated and oversaw the hardest-to-crack cases in western region of USA when she wasn't busy mentoring the brightest of the upcoming officers and detectives. She was a legend.

When Patrick arrived, he was shown to her office on the top floor of the building. Linda Barnes got up and held out her hand, welcoming Patrick. She emphasized her preference for being called by her first name after decades of being 'Mrs. Barnes' out of respect—and habitual formality.

Linda was of middle height and average build. She was the spitting image of British actress Judy Dench, with her short, grayish hair, softly curved eyebrows, and the mild, controlled smile reflecting wisdom and compassion. She wore very little make up.

The office was, as Patrick had expected, both spacious, uncluttered, and impressive. The most striking feature was that everything was placed in an angle, with furniture, rugs, and decor matching in style and color.

Linda gestured to Patrick to take a seat. They sat down at the circular conference table—no 'end of the table for the boss,' Patrick thought. 'No one doubts who's in charge.'

Patrick put out stacks of production records, RI-credit slips from IRS and EPA, financial records, and Hannah's list of 75 deals with the names and companies that were customers of Gooding Bioenergy.

"Were do we start?" Linda asked without looking at the papers.

Patrick explained what Katie has explained to him at their first meeting. "Here," Patrick tapped a finger on top of one pile, "is a letter to your office from Bryan Carlson dated December 19, 2013. He wanted to inform us about this matter, but there was no response. That was, obviously, before Bryan was killed," Patrick said with a hint of 'this-could-have-been-avoided-if-your-office-had-acted-promptly,' but he didn't say that. Linda sensed the jab but was most of all as shocked as Patrick had been.

"He was killed?"

"Yes! Blown up on Valentine's Day. You may remember the news about a car that blew up near Idaho Falls?"

"From the TV news, yes," Linda said and nodded.

"Actually, Bryan's car didn't *blow up*; it was *blown up*." Linda understood the distinction and nodded again. "And that was a mistake," Patrick continued, "if that's the right word, because the *target* of the killing—according to my thinking—was not the young man but a young woman, Katie Carlson, former member of the Toponis Order and an employee of the Gooding Bioenergy company. She's—eh, was — the wife of the victim."

"Jesus," Linda said and leaned back for a moment. "What a tragedy."

"Yes. Impossible to fathom: Newly married and losing your husband is tragic under all circumstances, but losing him under such circumstances must be horrible."

They sat pensively until Linda asked, "But why would anyone want to kill Katie Carlson?"

"I'm working on the theory that someone wanted Katie silenced because of *suspicions* that, one: There *was* a leak of damaging information about the operation of Gooding Bioenergy, and two: Katie was the source of the leaked information—which, of course, she was; that's why we have the documents in front of us. So, the person who had those suspicions was right about both issues . . . but didn't know that! The question is: Who guessed right, and who did something about it? So . . ."

"So, where do we start?" Linda said again.

"Let's start with defining what kind of practical tasks we have in front of us," Patrick said. "I don't have the jurisdiction to go outside my district, or at least outside Idaho if that should be necessary, but you guys do. So, I will focus on the murder case and the local players in and around the Toponis Order. You can focus on all the other business people in the transactions described in this material," he pointed on the pile of papers in front of them. "We don't know yet who's the big fish in this pond but two names stand out." McInnes pointed to the 'people folder.'

"Does that work for you? Or . . ."

"That's sound good. Let me bring two of our detectives into this meeting while we are planning all this." She got up and came back a few moments later with Detectives Jasmine White and Eddie Galway.

McInnes got up and shook hands with both detectives. When they all sat down, coffee was brought in. They spend a few minutes introducing themselves and the focus of their work.

Jasmine White was a tall woman, probably 5'11-6', with light brown skin, dark brown eyes, and full lips. Her well-coiffured afro hair framed her delicate, symmetrical features in an elegant way. Most people would think she was an exotic model. 'Nubian,' was the word that first came to Patrick's mind.

Eddie sat to her right. He was known as a fast talking, young man who exuded a high level of energy. He looked fit like a runner. He had thick, almost black hair, a well trimmed black beard, and full eyebrows curving over his narrow set eyes. The somewhat coarse features and tanned skin made many think of him as East-european. Despite Eddie's looks and because of his last name, Patrick guessed he was of Irish descent. 'Maybe something to chat about later?'

Linda gave a very brief overview of the matter. "I'll go into the details when Patrick McInnes has left. He doesn't need to hear me retelling his story," she added with a warm smile.

"Because we have a crime case in a addition to the economic crime, we need a new set of resources," Linda continued. "We, being a federal agency, should connect with IRA and EPS and ask them to be part of the team. They have a fraud unit—as you know—and they should be updated on everything we find, starting with the information in front of us. Who knows? They may already have some of these people in the crosshair.

"I'll take care of that part myself," Linda said.

The meeting lasted two more hours and the FBI detectives took a lot of notes. In closing, Linda said, "We should meet again next week, unless something forces us to move faster."

The same afternoon, she informed her staff and Patrick that she had confirmation from the fraud unit in IRS that they would come to her office for a briefing. 'Wow,' Patrick thought, 'that's promising.'

Before the day was over, Linda sent out a note "to all individuals in this Federal Investigation & Operation, to the effect that FBI in Washington, DC had asked her to coordinate the entire case. Subpoenas were underway to all investigators in the operation, so they had legal backup for obtaining any document needed in the case. She also prepared written gag-orders to any individual the team would be in contact with, emphasizing that discussing the case with anyone *other* than the person who had presented the gag order, would be considered 'tampering with and interfering in a federal investigation.'

Operation *Peregrine* was underway.

CHAPTER SIXTEEN

DETECTIVE PATRICK MCINNES CALLED KATIE after arriving back in Idaho Falls. They decided to meet next day at the library, "our field operation office," he said with a boyish laughter.

When they sat down in Katie's little office in the back of the library, Patrick reported from the meeting with Linda Barnes and her team.

"I'm curious about these two guys who keep coming up in many of the transactions of Gooding Bioenergy," Patrick said "Ron Patterson and Dan Hancock. What do you know about them?"

"They were top sales representatives. Actually, Ron Patterson is on the payroll. I don't know much other than he was a top notch guy. I met him a few times when he was in Idaho for special events. Quiet, professional, and a very nice guy. Avid golfer, by the way.

"The other one, Hancock . . . I never met him but he's an independent rep with his own company. He was both a buyer and a broker of oil deals. There was a lot of contact with him in Isaiah's office as far as I could tell. I could probably get Hannah to find some of it."

"Well, we have his name and some of this contact information on the sheet she already gave us, so let me start there. I'll ask some of the FBI field guys to start with Hancock, find him—I think he was in Atlanta, right?"—Katie nodded—"and ask him about his business. I'll give them my ten cents worth of knowledge about B99 and all that stuff so they don't make a fool of themselves."

#

"Can I come over?" Patrick asked when he called.

'Wow, that was quick,' Katie thought. 'I thought he said a couple of days. But sure, why not?' Katie smiled.

She liked Patrick. He was so *unbwogable*—one of the few Kiswahili words Katie remembered from a book about an African tribal king she had read in high school. Nothing can *bwogo* him—bother him. He always appeared so unruffled and he had had a calming effect on Katie from the moment she met him.

"Yes, *Sir*. Any time." They both laughed.

"Thanks, my Lady."

She had tea ready when he arrived. They sat down. Katie immediately knew there was some kind of trouble on the horizon.

"Dan Hancock is dead," Patrick started, "and the . . ."

"Oh my God," Katie exclaimed. "He wasn't that old, or sick, as far as I know."

"Car accident. About three-to-four weeks ago; January 20 to be precise. According to the local police and the report my people obtained from them, he was traveling alone in a wooded area southwest of Atlanta when his car apparently failed to follow a curve and crashed into a tree."

Katie was stunned and lost for words.

"The police has been investigating the accident. There was no alcohol or drugs found in the body. The car was relatively new. The tracks didn't suggest high speed. It was a very low-traffic area. It was a cold night but not icy. So . . . "

"What was it then?"

It dawned on her the moment she said it. She put three fingers over her mouth as if to suppress a sob, holding her breath.

"Foul play?" she whispered.

"That's what the local police think.

"I just came from a meeting with Matthew and Isaiah. Since they were Hancock's business partners, and Hancock was single with no family that we know of at this time, I thought it was the appropriate thing to do. There really wouldn't be another way that Gooding Bioenergy would find out—for a short while, that is."

"Of course," Katie said with a thin voice. "How was the reaction there?"

"They were both shocked but Matthew was extremely upset. He honestly looked like he'd seen a ghost. But they didn't say anything other than, you know, the usual comments in a situation like that."

"I see."

They both sat in silence, sipping tea and eating Oreos.

"But you know what?" Patrick said. "What bothers the heck out of me is . . . is the fact they didn't say anything *in particular.*"

"What do you mean? What was there to say other than . . .?"

"They didn't wonder why a police officer in Little Falls knows about a car accident in Atlanta."

"I didn't think about it either," Katie said with a crooked smile. "Shouldn't I have wondered?"

"Not really. You *know* I'm on a team that investigates the biofuel fraud cases. They don't.

"So, I wonder if Mathew and Isaiah suspected Hancock was dead or maybe even *knew* . . ." Patrick stopped. "Now, *that* would be interesting. Let me get back to that. So, the shock was about the fact I and FBI officers are involved in a traffic acci . . . Sorry, too many loose ends. Let me think this through." He ran his fingers through the reddish hair.

Katie frowned as she wrestled with all Patrick's information.

"Why would it be interesting if they had expec . . . Oh, I see. In that case, there might have been threats against Hancock, and Matthew would have been aware of the threats."

"Geez man! I'll ask my boss to hire you. You think faster than many of my people." Katie almost got up to give him a kiss but he already stood and explained he needed to be on his way.

"Now, if there's any substance to these thoughts, there's even more reasons for you to be careful about your whereabouts."

"Do I need a bodyguard?" Katie joked but frowned as she realized that she might indeed need one.

Patrick shook his head lightly as if he was going to say that she already had him. 'But she 's right. She needs protection.'

He hugged Katie lightly on the way out.

#

"What the Hell happened," Matthew blurted out when he called Nicolas.

"About what?"

"About Hancock."

"What about him?"

"You know what. You said he was not in the business anymore, but . . ."

"Which he isn't!"

"You're damned right he isn't. And he's not on vacation either. He's dead."

"I should have said 'a very long vacation,' I guess."

"D'you think this is a laughing matter? Did you have a role in this traffic accident?"

"You're moving into a dangerous territory, my friend," Nicolas said in a warning tone. "How are you even being informed about a traffic accident in rural Georgia?"

"Oh, so you know it was in *rural* Georgia? He lived in a southwest Atlanta. But to answer your question: The Idaho police showed up in our offices to inform us about Hancock because we were business partners and Dan doesn't have any family. I didn't ask them why they were informed about it, but I can add two and two, and it appears to me that the accident must have been serious and suspicious enough for the police in Georgia to be in touch with the police here. Who knows, maybe it is even FBI?"

"And did you ask them how they knew Hancock was your business partner?"

"Of course not. You may not have high regards for the police, but they're not stupid. This happened in January. I'm pretty sure they spent the time to figure out what business he was in, including who his business partners are—or were, rather. And we were among them."

Nicolas was quiet for a moment, thinking about the ramification of the situation. "Matt," he finally said, "we're well protected under our umbrella. I'll check with some guys in California if anything's going on in their circles. If there is, we'll know it before anything gets out of control.

"So, don't worry, but don't let your guards down either."

CHAPTER SEVENTEEN

THE FOLLOWING WEEK, PATRICK McINNES was back in Salt Lake City to a *Peregrine* team meeting. Detectives Jasmine White and Eddie Galway had just gotten back from Santa Monica, where they had been 'scouting.'

"What did we learn in California?" Linda asked as she started the meeting. "Eddie, will you go first?"

"Sure. It was an eye-opener," Eddie said. "At first, we both met with Ron Patterson. A very nice, very experienced guy, who clearly has been successful in the fuel business. He has been with Gooding Bioenergy for a number of years and knows Matthew Smith well. He also knows Nicolas d'Aubert, if that's his real name, of course; we'll get back to that. Ron and Nicolas have met a couple of times and spoken occasionally by phone as their businesses have developed over the past few years.

"Then we split up. I went to see some of the *Sirius* operations, and Jasmine went to meet with the gentleman who hosted a dinner party where Nicolas was a guest.

"I got a picture of an apparently extremely successful fuel operation with networks throughout USA and in several places in Europe. Nicolas is constantly on the move, constantly making deals. He must have not one but many Rolodex files—"digital, of course," he added when Linda looked like she would say 'no way' about Rolodex.

"People speak well about him, perhaps more out of respect than anything else. An extravagant life style with sports cars, yachts, and airplanes always make for respect and admiration. A few people referred to his quick temper and his bodyguards. No one explained why they are needed, but it could be part of a cultivated image or just the fact that the rich and famous do feel they need protection from harassment.

"Anyway, everything seemed clean and respectable. But Jasmine got a different impression."

Linda turned to Jasmine.

"I did indeed. I met with the Adamses who had hosted a dinner a few years ago that included Nicolas d'Aubert. Out of pure curiosity and an interest in people, places, and history, Mr. Adams—who's a retired publishing executive, by the way—looked into the story and background of *Marquis Nicolas d'Aubert, Toulon, France.* That's the reading on his business card. Long story short: There's no such family in Aix-en-Provence where Nicolas claimed to be from. Or anywhere else in France. And there's no castle, no noble family. It's pure fabrication. Mr. Adams didn't look further into to places where Nicolas claimed to have done business or into the marinas where he has his yachts, called *Sirius.* Those places are Santa Monica and Larnaca on Cyprus.

"In addition, Mr. Adams found out from a local friend in LAPD that Nicolas has been investigated numerous times for improper business operations—without being indicted, though.

"Mr. Adams also said his family does not see Nicolas any more, since they know he's phony, and to their knowledge, none of their neighbors do either.

"The big question is, of course: What else is phony about him? My guess is that it's probably everything. The guy exists, but what's known about him is all based on his own fabrications."

"Wow," Linda said. "So, where does that leave us in regards to the murder case and the tax fraud case?"

"We *may* even have two murder cases," Patrick said, looking at Linda, "if we include the Georgia car accident in January we learned about the other day. But for my part, the Idaho Falls murder case is clear cut. We believe we have a motive. Although we don't have a suspect as of right now, we can easily think of several people having a reason to silence Katie, and that those suspects are directly linked to the fraud case."

Linda nodded her agreement and said, "If we are correct about the assumptions we mentioned just now, what's next?"

There was a moment of silence before Patrick said, "I think we should scrutinize some of the transactions between Gooding Bioenergy and this Nicolas-guy. Katie has already given us names of people involved in their last seventy-five transactions as well as details of a number of those deals. You have that information already." Linda nodded. "We also need to get to the banks of all these people and their companies. That will be a matter for IRS. It may well be outside the country, but IRS know whom to go to."

Linda nodded while she took notes.

"If need be and if you twist my arm, I'll go to Turkey, or was it Cyprus? Lacarnos or something? And snoop around." Jasmine White added with a coquettish smile, which created lighthearted laughter.

"I bet you will," Linda said.

"I'll carry your suitcase," Eddie offered.

"Enough, you two!"

Linda pretended to be serious but her smile gave away that she was amused as well. It was Linda's philosophy that just like in a hospital operating room, you have to have a sense of humor and let off some steam during long, intense cases. The same applies to detectives's work, she always said. 'And this is a complex case, or set of cases,' Linda reasoned.

"Listen, here's what I have made notes of."

Linda started counting them off on her fingers.

"One! We have a murder case in Idaho Falls, dated February 14th. Patrick is in charge and I will allocate FBI support to the case to the extent needed. I'm the contact for that.

"Two! We have a suspicious car accident southwest of Atlanta involving Dan Hancock. It dates back to January 20th. Eddie, being the perennial NASCAR enthusiast, will be in charge of that and get the FBI support to the extent needed. I'm the contact for that, too.

"Three! We have pretty good evidence that numerous biofuel transactions involving Gooding Bioenergy and this Nicolas-guy were fraudulent. That will be the responsibility of IRS's fraud department. I'll contact them and Patrick will coordinate the information flow with the input of Katie and others, I suppose." Patrick nodded.

"Four! We need to put a protective shadow on Katie so nothing happens to her. If she was the target of the bombing, that risk hasn't gone away. On the contrary, I'd say.

"Five! We need to put tails on Nicolas and Matthew to see their every move."

Linda sat back. "That's it from my side," she said. "Anything else?"

"I think we need to add Isaiah to number five," Patrick said. "He may only be a paper pusher in the sense that he did not actually make any deals, but he would still have been knowledgeable about all of it, and as CFO he's responsible for filing reports with IRS; fraudulent report, that is. And just one more thing to keep in the back of our minds: Nicolas has bodyguards. There could be a reason for that besides the vanity-factor. He may use brute force to get people to comply with their own rules."

"Very good," Linda said. "As this case builds up, a lot of information needs to be coordinated. That's *my* primary responsibility besides opening doors within FBI, IRS, EPA and the judicial systems for subpoenas, gags, and so on. In short, easing the process of bringing these five activities together.

"I'd like to meet in about a week depending on how much progress we make in the meantime. I have an idea for how we can tighten the rope around these people. I'll explain that at another meeting," Linda said as she adjourned the meeting.

CHAPTER EIGHTEEN

PATRICK CALLED KATIE TO SEE if she would be available for a briefing from the meeting with FBI the day before.

"Sure, I'm around. When do you want to meet?"

"If tea is an option, I'll be happy to accept your invitation for this afternoon," he said, chuckling.

"Ah, let me check my calendar," Katie said, trying to sound very businesslike. "Oh, darn! It's gonna be . . . No, wait a sec! I guess I'm open in about five to ten minutes." She smiled.

"I'll be there in seven-eight," Patrick said.

When Katie opened the door, she noticed there was no police car outside. "Did you walk over here?" she teased him.

"I'm in an unmarked police cruiser. I parked a block away."

"Like a secret lover?" Katie couldn't help teasing Patrick and they both started to laugh.

"Almost. Well, I'll explain that in a sec."

They went into the living room, where Katie had set out on the coffee table a British style tea pot and two cups—'no mugs,' Patrick noticed—and Danish Butter Cookies in the famous, circular tin.

"I was in Salt Lake City yesterday for a meeting with the Utah chief of FBI, and . . . "

"I know," Katie injected nonchalantly.

"What? You do?" Patrick was flabbergasted. "How . . ?" When Katie bursted out laughing, he sat back and joined in the laugh. 'She's a trip,' he thought.

"So, you know that, uh? What did we talk about?"

"Me."

After more laughter, Patrick managed to get serious. "Actually, you're right. We did talk about you—among other things. Five issues no less, and you are directly involved in two of them." Patrick outlined the five issues that Linda had summarized and finished, "so, number one: We need to get as much information on Matthew and Isaiah as possible, including the deals they're making these days, the reports they file, and the tax credits they receive as they go forward. Can you organize that?"

Katie ruffled her short, black hair with her left hand as she reflected on the tasks involved in getting inside the Order through Hannah.

"It'll take a little time," Katie said. "But yes, I can do that. What's the other thing?"

"This is risky business, as you know first hand. So, we—and that means the Idaho Falls police department—need to put a protective shadow on you. We all agree you're the target of some person or persons, whomever it may be, who will use force to silence you. I don't think they have given up on getting to you, although that *is* guesswork." He noticed the frown on Katie's face and added, "I'm sorry to put it so bluntly. But we can't take that chance."

"That's OK. I was actually going to ask you about that. What does it mean to put a shadow on me. Practically speaking, I mean."

"We will have one officer at all times, around the clock—not the same person all the time, of course—watching *you* when you are outside the *house* and watching the house all the time, whether you are there or not." Katie nodded in silence. Patrick could see a question was forming in her mind, so he added, "the officer will not be *in* your house, unless you call for it.

"Also, I'd prefer you do not go anywhere in a car," Patrick added.

"That won't be hard. I don't have one," she said with a sad smile.

"Well, that's the other thing. When you do need to go somewhere, we'll have an unmarked police cruiser at your disposal."

"Wow, I get to have my own police car?"

"Nah, not quite. An officer will be driving."

"Female?"

"Sure, if you wish. I just need a one-day notice."

"Anything else?"

"It would be the best thing if you keep changing your daily schedule. Most people follow a set pattern every single day, but that's a very risky because that makes you an easy target. Change the time and the route when you go to work, to the gym, go shopping, et cetera. Make your weekly schedule unpredictable for an outsider. And be observant of your surroundings, people and cars. Report anything to me that you find unusual. Even the smallest of things can be important."

"Very well." Katie went through in her mind what she had learned in the past 30 minutes. "I have two questions," she said.

"OK."

"How do I communicate with you. We can't fill up the books in the library with notes to one another," she said, smiling.

"You are one step ahead of me; an annoying habit," Patrick said with a chuckle, "but here's the answer. I have a burner phone here," he pulled it out of his inside pocket and handed it to Katie. "It has a bunch of garbage phone numbers in it, but my direct line is Rick. It has a one-touch call button. I'll get a couple of other burner phones, one at the time, so we can switch regularly. I have all your numbers but you will only need one number for me. It is a secure line. It will be recorded, by the way, so don't . . . "

". . . say anything improper," Katie finished Patrick's sentence, cocking her head.

"Pretty much, yes. But, more importantly, don't say *anything* that identifies who you are and where you are. I already know it's you when you call. And never say your name."

"Is that it?"

"Almost. One more thing. We will put shadows on Matthew and Isaiah, too. Not for protection but for information gathering. And in addition to that, we need Hannah's help. Since she lives with Matthew that represents some challenges, but . . ."

"She *wants* to help. And I trust her one-hundred percent. Actually, she's the only person in the Order I ever trusted . . . and even liked. She's a gem."

"Good. I hope to meet her soon. Oh, and we'll put a shadow on Nicolas, too, of course, but that's outside my territory.

"That's all, but you knew that, I understand." Patrick managed to keep the brewing laughter under control.

Patrick got up. "I need to get going."

"Time for one more question?" Katie asked.

"Sure. Shoot."

"Is it OK if your name for the burner calls could be Macki instead of Rick?"

"I guess so. But, uhm, why?"

"Hannah and I already call you that, so it will be easier for me."

"Seriously? Why Macki? . . . Oh, I get it. Yes, I'll make a note on that."

On the way out, Katie asked, "One very, *very* last thing. When is all this shadowing going to start?"

"Right now." When I get back to the station, I'll send a shadow over here to watch the house. He or she, as it may be, will follow you if you go somewhere."

"I won't."

Patrick gave Katie a hug. "You are a trouper," he said, holding her a moment longer than she expected, and left.

After reflecting on what Patrick had told her, Katie texted Hannah.

> *Met Macki. Very helpful.*
> *MM@UPThree tm.*

Hannah knew Katie's codes for 'meet me,' at the 'usual place at 3 pm' and the 'tomorrow,' and she sent a tacit CFM-H for 'Confirmed - Hannah' reply back a few minutes later.

When Hannah and Katie met the next day, Katie explained the action plan that Patrick had laid out.

Hannah was a bit overwhelmed but confirmed that she could and would do her part of the work.

CHAPTER NINETEEN

LINDA CONTACTED THE CHIEF of Police in Atlanta.

"As far as we understand, you guys consider the car accident near Chattahoochee involving Dan Hancock a potential crime. I read the initial reports and would like to send one of my people over to you to coordinate and exchange information between our task forces, if you can agreed to that?" Linda started.

"Absolutely. Your people will be most welcome. Anything that can move this case forward should be pursued. How soon can you have someone come over?"

"Tomorrow would be fine. I'll send detective Eddie Galway. He actually has a background as a NASCAR racer, so he's nuts about cars and how they function. He even said he had an idea. So he's the right man. He can be there just before lunch."

"Excellent. If he sends the flight information, I'll have Larry Hartman meet Eddie at the airport."

#

"Summarize for me what you have at this time," Eddie said when the two detectives drove from Hartsfield Airport towards the police headquarters in Atlanta."

"Briefly," Larry Hartman started, "Hancock was not DUI—neither drugs, alcohol, or sedatives. The impact on the tree the car crashed into and the lack of breaking tracks on the road suggest he went at moderate speed but still failed to negotiate the curve."

"How about tires and the car's general condition?"

"The car was a one year old Toyota Corolla, so it was in good shape. Brake pads, too. It was a cold night indeed, but unusually good road conditions for that time of the year and for that location—wooded, that is. So, the possibility that he slid off the road because he went too fast or it was icy is zero, in my opinion. And that adds to the puzzling thing that there were no signs of brake tracks. I mean, if he had gone too fast for the conditions, he would have tried to stop or slow down the car, right?"

Eddie nodded as his agreement with Larry's conclusion. "Where is the car wreck, by the way?"

"At a local junk yard. It was taken there the morning after the accident, which was on January 20 at 1 a.m., by the way.

"That's more than a month ago! Don't go to the office. Let's go to the junk yard right away."

"It's totaled. There's nothing to . . ." Larry Hartman said, incredulity creeping into his voice. Before he could ask 'why,' Eddie said, "'Totaled' is an insurance term for 'not worth fixing;' but you and I probably wouldn't call it a total wreck, so, there are still many useful and intact parts on it. That's why junk yards love to have them, by the way. And what we want is the car's computer."

"O-Kay" he said slowly, revealing he had no idea what for. He got off of I-85 and onto the road to the junk yard. "On the way, explain what you think we can learn from that."

Eddie explained that modern cars have computers that keep a record of all the operating functions, "you know, like the black box that are retrieved from airplane wrecks. It will still be intact. And when we access it from my laptop," Eddie added, "we can analyze the data and see what happened—from a mechanical point of view."

They found the place in a workshop district of Northern Atlanta and went to someone looking like a foreman. Despite showing their badges, describing the car, and showing its licence plate number, Eddie and Larry were met with a lot of resistance. Everything from 'I don't think we have that car anymore' to 'I can't let you touch the car' was attempted.

Eddie lost his patience. He stepped very close to the foreman, leaned into his comfort zone, and rested his dark eyes him, eyebrows almost meeting as he frowned. "Don't make me wait a minute longer or you will be under arrest." The foreman stepped aside and let Eddie and Larry inspect the car wreckage.

"We need your mechanic to remove the car's computer," Larry said, and before the foreman had a chance to object, Eddie added, "Take us to the owner of this place."

Although there was a customer window in the small wooden shack, Eddie went inside. There were papers, scissors, tools, and stacks of books everwhere. A waste basket filled with empty Coke cans and a mug on the window-sill with day-old coffee completed the mess. To call it 'a chaos' would be a compliment.

Eddie explained what they needed. After being presented with the subpoena and gag order, and after some serious huffing and puffing, the owner accepted, got up, and ordered one of the mechanics to remove the computer from behind the engine room. Ten minutes later, Eddie and Larry were on their way back.

After a late lunch and with mugs of steaming coffee on the table, the two detectives huddled over the car's computer. Larry White was still at a loss about the possible outcome, and his mind soon wandered off.

Until Eddie literally jumped in his seat.

"Holy smokes," Eddie said. He double-checked his finding. "The car didn't brake."

"Why would it all of a sudden . . .?"

"The computer was tampered with! Hacked without a doubt. !"

"Hacked? How d'you . . . You said that before. Explain how that works." Larry White was now genuinely curious.

"It's along story, but the short version is this: All major car functions are controlled via servo-motors, meaning, for instance, that the foot's pressure on the brake pedal is translated into a command to the servo-motor that activates the brakes with a force that is proportional to the foot pressure on the pedal. In old days you had to apply a lot of pressure to stop a car; now a small motor does the work for you. Same with steering. Obviously, if the servo motors are *disabled*, the brakes will not get the 'command' to break.

"And these functions can be disabled and taken over by pretty much any modern computer—if you know what you're doing. And see . . . "Eddie stopped talking and pointed to his screen, "the brakes stopped working at 1:09 a.m. on Monday, January 20. And look . . . So was the steering! Dan had no way of salvaging the situation when he realized he could not stop the car."

"Jeez. Yes, I see. D'you want to go to the accident scene?" Larry Hartman asked after digesting the information.

"Depends. Was there a scene report with photos?"

"Sure, of course. We have them in the file."

"Then we don't have to go. What the photos will show is much better than what the accident scene looks like now, a month later."

Eddie poured himself another cup of coffee while Larry Hartman went to fetch the case file. A few minutes later and with a dozen photos spread out on the table, they both looked carefully at all of them in silence. Then Larry said, "No break tracks, no careening tracks, nothing to suggest that the driver tried to salvage the situation. He just . . . ran off the road in the curve."

"My words exactly," Eddie said.

"Any other possible explanation?"

"Sure," Eddie said, "the driver could've fallen asleep or been unconscious, or someone could—manually—have steered the car off the . . . nah, unless the driver was defenseless there would've been a struggle and that would have shown up in the tracks. My take on this situation is *not* to look for other explanations until this 'hacking lead' is pursued to a conclusion."

"Which is: *Who* hacked the car's computer. And why?" Larry articulated the open questions.

"Exactly. And since this disabling of the car has to be done in real time in order to work, the hacker must have been quite close to the accident site, waiting for the car to come by. And it would also have to be someone who had accessed the car's computer before, since you can't do that in the amount of time it drives by you."

"That's going to be a needle-in-the-haystack search."

"I know. And we need other people involved in that that search. But I have an idea about that."

#

Eddie White was inspired by the discovery. He knew the task to find the hacker was a daunting one, so on the plane home later that night, he scribbled a list of questions that needed to be answered. He made a list of people he could think of—and even some that were pulled out of the blue.

And then he added his idea.

CHAPTER TWENTY

JASMINE WHITE GOT HER WISH.

Two days after the *Peregrine* meeting, she flew to Nicosia, the capital of Cyprus. She had gotten a lot of names of locals on Cyprus where Nicolas claimed to have lived; and she had names of people Nicolas had dropped during his conversations with Mr. Adams and Ron Patterson; and finally, she had names from Katie and Hannah's list, too. She would be busy.

Jasmine had never been to any of the Mediterranean countries before, so she spent the weekend soaking up the atmosphere of the coastal cities and decided not to go back to Nicosia until Monday morning. 'A lot of Nicolas's contacts would be boaters and sailors and possibly easy to find in marinas. And with his reputation, someone might know him well—maybe I can even find Nicolas's yacht there, too.'

At every location she went to, Jasmine visited marina dock masters, sailors with large yachts, hotels, fine restaurants, jewelers, and even churches and banks. No one knew of Nicolas d'Aubert in Paphos, Limassol, Famagusta, or in Lanarca. She concluded that if he indeed spent time on Cyprus, he was not known by that last name. She changed strategy. When she asked for a yacht by the name of *Sirius*, people in Lanarca lightened up.

"Oh yes, Nick loves it here. The other marinas are too touristy but Lanarca seems to suit his idea about a good facility and privacy."

Asked about details, everyone admitted they didn't know all that much about the owner of *Sirius*. No one knew his last name. "You know, some people don't need a last name," some of them said good-humorously. "Like Elvis. Or Pelé. Or Madonna."

Others talked about Nick coming and going. "He seems to be doing a lot of business here, though." But there were still no specifics.

But Jasmine got lucky. *Sirius 2* was docked at the Lanarca marina, taking up almost the entire length of a pier. Jasmine sat down on a bench and just looked at it. It seemed deserted but she was sure it wasn't. 'One must make a ton of money to be able to afford an ocean liner like that,' she mused. The sun felt good on her back, and the Zerphyr-like ocean breeze filled with seagull chatter had a salty freshness to it. She could sit there for hours, she thought, but eventually got up and started to walk back to her rental car.

"Miss?" someone called her.

Jasmine turned and pointed a finger towards herself, gesturing 'me?'

"Yes, you. What are you doing here?"

Jasmine contemplated how to deal with him. He was at least 6'4", clean-shaven and with playboy-style long, light-brown hair. His tan spoke about a life in the sun and the surf. Broad like a refrigerator, he looked like he could handle every situation. 'Perhaps a wrestler,' she thought, 'but definitely an Adonis.' He eyed Jasmine from top to toe and back up, stopping a couple of times on the way. She was used to attention but not that much; then again, she imagined her looks stood out even more in Europe than at home.

She decided to play it cool and unaffected.

"Nothing. What are you doing?"

"Taking care of the yacht. And you?" he repeated.

"Looking at her. Seems like you're doing a good job. Taking care of her would keep any owner busy." Jasmine was curious to see what kind of reaction her deliberate mistake would prompt.

"Owners of yachts like this don't take care of them," he said haughtily.

"I guess not. Well, I won't keep you from doing your job. Boss must be coming soon." She took the first step to move away again.

"Just left. Won't be here for several months."

That was an unnecessary volunteering of information by a person who seemed on guard. Jasmine wondered if it was a slip of the tongue or if it—in his mind—was totally unimportant. 'Of course, why would a casual stanger care about when the owner would be around?' Jasmine thought.

"Do you want to look around onboard?" the yacht keeper said with a sudden friendly voice. He was definitely not a steward, most likely not the captain either. Jasmine decided he was one of Nicolas's many bodyguards.

"I'm on my way to Famagusta but I might be back tomorrow after a meeting in Nicosia. Thanks, though."

"I'll have lunch ready." He put two fingers to his cap as a salute and went back onboard. When she reached the end of the pier, she looked over her shoulder and saw the man in the stern, looking after her.

#

Linda had set up a meeting with the president of the Republic Bank of Cyprus in Nicosia, Mr. Kostas Demetriou, so mid Monday morning, Jasmine went to see him.

After some small talk about this divided Greek/Turkish island-country and everything from climate and tourism to the upcoming election, Jasmine put the main issue on the table.

"We are looking into the banking transactions of one of your clients, Mr. Nicolas d'Aubert. He's a resident of U.S.A. but frequently visits Cyprus."

"Yes, that's what Mrs. Barnes said, but as I explained to her, we don't have a customer of that name."

Jasmine had expected that answer. "But you *do* know of him?"

"No. As a matter of fact, I've never heard of a Mr. Nicolas d'Aubert," Demetriou said.

"Do you know that he has a very large yacht in the Larnaca marina called *Sirius*?"

"Well, since I don't know him, I couldn't poss . . ."

"Let me rephrase that: Do you know who owns the yacht *Sirius 2* which is docked in the Larnaca marina?"

"No, I don't." Demetriou didn't show any subtle signs of a person lying under pressure. She decided to increase it.

"I was at the marina last night. Lanarca, that is. A lot of people there have heard about the *Sirius 2*. And they also talked about the business transactions Mr. d'Aubert does on this island. Given the size of the yacht, I'd venture a guess that Mr. d'Aubert is a very wealthy man. Bank presidents usually know very wealthy people in relatively small places, like Monaco or Lichtenstein, et cetera, wouldn't you agree?"

"That may be right. I have no idea who bank presidents know or don't know, but I don't know Mr. d'Aubert."

"So, this front page photo in the *'i Kypros'* from a few years ago of you and a gentleman named *Marquis d'Aubert* does't ring a bell?"

Jasmine push a newspaper clipping across the table and expected a stunned reaction.

Demetriou slowly nodded. "I did meet that man, yes, but his name was *not* d'Aubert."

"What was his last name?"

"Ionesco," Demetriou said without a moment of reflection. "Nicolas Ionesco."

"And you do business with him?"

"Yes. Irregularly, but at times a lot."

"International?"

"Yes, almost all of it," Demetriou said.

"Countries, cities?"

"USA mostly and Turkey second-most."

"Cities?"

"Los Angeles, Houston, New York and only Istanbul in Turkey—as far as I remember.

"And Nicosia, of course," he added.

"I'm sure Mrs. Barnes told you I have a subpoena with me from FBI and IRS for accessing the accounts of this Mr. Ionescu."

"Well, I don't want to be a contrarian," Demetriou said with a gleeful smile, "but you don't have a subpoena for *that* man there. You have it for a Mr. d'Aubert, who's not our customer."

Jasmine knew this was technically correct. "I'll have that tomorrow. I thank you for your time. I'll go back to Lanarca now but I'll meet you again before I fly back," Jasmine said as she got up and shook hands with the bank president.

On the way out, she stopped at the Ladies Room, dropped a small metal box into the trash can under paper towels and used pads. 'No one's gonna look there and cleaning will probably not be until early tomorrow morning,' she thought, 'and that's time enough.'

As Jasmine walked out of Republic Bank of Cyprus, she weighed the risks against the rewards of going back to Lanarca and have lunch on the yacht. She could be a sitting duck or be taken hostage, she could be trapped into a forced sexual situation when alone with a stranger, but she could, on the other hand, also learn something very interesting. She had a slim hand gun in her jacket pocket and a powerful miniature taser in her pants pocket. She could defend herself quite well. But if the guard was not alone, she could be . . . trapped.

She decided to go for it.

CHAPTER TWENTY-ONE

"WELCOME," THE GUARD SAID, AS he held out his hand to Jasmine when she showed up on the pier in the Lanarca marina. "I should introduce myself. I'm Thomas."

"I'm Laura," Jasmine said.

Thomas led Jasmine up the boarding ramp onto the rear deck, where lunch was set out for two people. It struck Jasmine that there was something almost obnoxiously arrogant about being so sure she would return, that he already had prepared lunch for two. Still, there was something charming about it, too. Jasmine was intrigued.

"Let me show you around," Thomas said and took Jasmine around the upper deck facilities and the bigger salons belowdeck. It was a magnificent yacht, just as Jasmine had expected. It was spotless, tastefully decorated, and amply furnished. It had an entertainment room next to the living room, several bedrooms and bathrooms, and even a small swimming pool on the rear deck. 'A pool on a yacht,' Jasmine thought. 'Why would anyone do that?'

"Let's have a bite. I organized it the Cypriot way. I hope that meets your taste. Do you prefer white or red wine?"

"White, please."

Jasmine looked around again, nodding her appreciation. "I could certainly get used to a life on a boat like this. Yacht, excuse me."

Thomas acknowledged the correction with a gentle nod. 'He has style,' Jasmine thought. 'Not exactly what I'd expect from a bodyguard. Of course, he hasn't said he was a bodyguard.'

After a sip of wine, and the fist few bites of caviar on crackers, Jasmine asked, "So, what *do* you do on this yacht besides inviting and entertaining unknown visitors? Do you shop, cook, and clean?"

Thomas started laughing. "Gosh, no! Although I *live* on the yacht, we have staff for all that."

"So, what *is* your job here? Professional snorkeling?" They both laughed.

"I mean, what does Nicolas ask you to do?" Jasmine clarified.

The mentioning of Nicolas startled Thomas and he immediately steered the conversation away from that.

"Keep the yacht ready for when the boss wants to go sailing. That's all," he said with a wide smile. "So, tell me, what is Laura doing here, this far away from . . . from whereever you live in the U.S.?"

"Right now I'm in Idaho, taking care of family, but I'm originally from Boston. I'll go back there again one day. I miss the East coast."

"And are you on vacation here?"

"No, I'm here on an assigment. Working."

"What *do* you do for a living, if I may ask?"

"I'm a free lance journalist and writer with in interest in history. I'm here to get information about the Green Line. You know the . . ."

"Ah, the fiftieth anniversary of the 1974?"

Jasmine laughed. "Well, we haven't quit gotten to 2024, have we?" she said with a smile. "But it was originally started in 1964 and that's what some think of as the start—myself included, by the way—althought it was the *lengthening* across the entire island in 1974 that most people refer to as the anniversary. So, I wanted to interview people about how they live with the division today. If people even pay any attention to it anymore, that is. I guess I could start with you."

Thomas spoke in general terms about the Green Line, clearly not knowing a whole lot about it, and not being a Cypriot, not caring a whole lot either. Jasmine took a few notes while they talked, and it was clear to Jasmine that Thomas was as fake as Laura was, so by changing the subject, she wanted to put him on the spot.

"So, what kind of business do you guys do with Mr. Demetriou at the Republic Bank in Nicosia?"

That did throw Thomas off for a moment, and he chose the safe answer.

"I don't know Mr. Demet . . . or whatever."

"Really? But you talked with him on the phone just a few hours ago. And he called you Stan, by the way, not Thomas. And he told you I was heading back here to Lanarca after my meeting with him."

Stan was totally stunned. 'How in the world would she know that? He used a private line. She must have had help. But who? Demetriou himself—double-crossing us? No way. He's one of our own.' Stan needed the upper hand in the conversation and decided to turn the table on Jasmine.

"Is that so?" He paused. "So, what is Jasmine White doing here?"

That didn't surprise Jasmine at all, which in fact startled Stan and made him even more suspicious.

"I'm a free lance journalist and writer with in interest in history. I'm here to get information about the Green Line. You know . . ."

"Cut the bullshit, Jasmine. I heard something about FBI and subpoenas." He got up from the table and went behind Jasmine's chair. "Get up," he commanded, and started pulling the chair away under her. Jasmine rose. "Hand me the gun in your jacket." Jasmine took it out and handed it to Stan but left the jacket on the back of the chair. He put the gun in his own pocket and took a firm grip on Jasmine's upper left arm.

"Let's go downstair," he commanded.

"I don't think that's a good idea," Jasmine said calmly.

"Doesn't matter what you think."

"I was actually more concerned about *your* safety, not mine," Jasmine provoked.

Stan ignored the comment. "Start walking."

"Not wise, but if you insist!" She showed no fear. That, too, surprised Stan.

Stan forcefully guided Jasmine to the stairs that led to a salon downstairs. He pulled her to a stop when they got into a small, plush, all-red colored boudoir. He shut the door with his foot, which left the room almost dark. Stan stood closely behind her and put his hands on her shoulders as if to keep her still. Jasmine put her hand in the left pocket of her trousers. Stan wrapped one arm across her breasts and moved the other hand down towards her belly. 'The prelude to rape, or perhaps just intimidation?' Jasmine thought. Instead of stiffening up, she moved her right leg slightly to the right, widening her stance. Stan took advantage of that to press his hand in between her legs.

Jasmine shifted her weight slightly to the right, which forced Stan to shift his weight as well, not realizing that *he* now was keeping Jamine balanced on her left foot. When Jasmine knew Stan had his entire bodyweight on his right leg, she bent her right leg and slammed the foot backwards and hit Stan's kneecap with full force. She heard the splintering of the knee joint just before he collapsed on the floor, roaring in pain.

Jasmine pulled her left hand out of her pocket, spun around, and forced the high-powered taser onto the back of Stan. As the intense electrical current rushed through his body, Stan convulsed and crumbled in pain, trying to hit Jasmine who was behind him, then trying to no avail to protect himself. Jasmine kept the current flowing, and moments later he lost consciousness.

Jasmine put the taser in her pocket, went upstairs to the deck, grabbed her purse and jacket from the the chair, finished her white wine, and walked calmly down the ramp to the pier—and disappeared.

CHAPTER TWENTY-TWO

KATIE SOUNDED TERRIFIED WHEN SHE called Patrick McInnes from her burner phone. It was 11:30 at night.

"Someone was in my house a few minutes ago. I was asleep but heard . . ." She was gasping when she spoke. "The person disappeared through the backdoor when I got up."

"I'm on my way, eh, if that's OK?"

"Oh please, yes. And hurry."

Patrick cursed himself for having Katie's protective shadow observing her house only from the street side. 'We need to change that into a circling guard,' he thought, knowing he couldn't put two officers on the job. He drove as fast as he could without flashing red and blue lights, sirens, or markings on the car. He arrived in seven minutes.

Katie opened the door in her underwear and a T-shirt, went to the kitchen, and sat down on a chair with her knees pulled up to her chest. She looked like a small, injured bird, Patrick thought, when he followed her. "Let's get you out of here," Patrick said right away.

"I need to . . ."

"Put a pair of jeans and shoes on. We'll come back here tomorrow and get some of your clothes." In a matter of five minutes, they were out of the door.

"Where are we going?" Katie asked when they were in the car, speeding away.

"My place. We don't want to register your name anywhere for a room rent. I have a spare bedroom. Is that OK?"

"Anything works," Katie said in a tired voice.

It was a long, restless night and Katie was up before the break of dawn. Patrick had made the coffee machine ready to start brewing, so by the time Patrick got up, she had already helped herself to a second cup. She was about to apologize for that when Patrick said, "Glad you helped yourself. How did you sleep?"

"I didn't. Well, I guess one always dozes off at times, but . . ."

"I'll stay here this morning," Patrick said. "Later, we can go back to your house. Fix any damage, if necessary and . . ."

"Oh! My key! I forgot to bring the house key." She sighed and looked lost.

"Don't worry. We have people who knows how to get in without breaking windows or a doors."

Katie relaxed a bit. Patrick put his hand on hers, noticing how cold it was. "Take a long, hot shower. I'll have breakfast ready when you come out. Holler if there's anything you need."

"I'll, eh, actually, I need some, you know . . . I got my . . ."

"Use this for now," he said and pointed to a roll of soft paper towel, and added, "If you have at home what you need, we'll go there right after breakfast instead of later today. I'll call an assistant to meet us at your house."

Katie got up. "Thanks so much for taking me here." She stood in the doorway for a moment, lost again.

"You bet. Oh, it's right down the hall way, next to your room." He smiled when he said 'your room,' as if she had already moved in. When she disappeared, Patrick got up and started to make fried eggs easy-over, bacon, toasts, and cheeses. He put plates and a bowl out for cereal.

When she came out to the kitchen she looked refreshed and her big smile spread across her face when she saw the breakfast table. 'Man, she's pretty,' Patrick thought. They sat down and ate in silence, each absorbed in their own worlds.

'Life's full of twists and turns,' Patrick thought.

Katie thought of the unusual gestures of Patrick. And his kind considerations for what she needed. Can he extend such gestures to all the people he gets in contact with? Most would just do their job, even when doing it well. She wondered if there was a woman in his life. There were no signs in the apartment of a woman coming and going. Or a man, for that matter. It was bachelor-style, cosy, adequate, and comfortable but without the female touch in the decor or . . . 'or whatever women have in their homes.'

'Well, first things first,' she thought. We have a far more serious issue to deal with.'

"If you're done, let's go," Patrick said after a while. Katie smiled and nodded.

When they got to the house, the officer Patrick had called was already there. He had opened the front door and they went inside. Patrick and the officer scanned the entry ways into the house and saw the tell-tale signs of a lock that had been picked in the backdoor of the house. They went out into the small backyard and chatted while Katie gathered clothes, cosmetics, and toiletries and put it all into a suitcase.

"I'm done," she said ten minutes later. On they way out, she grabbed an extra pair of sneakers.

"Cash? Jewelry? Passport? Other important documents?" Patrick asked.

"What? Are we going out of the country?"

"No, but you don't want to leave anything of value behind. Or anything that is difficult to replace or that can limit your free movements for at least a week. Better safe than sorry." After another five minutes in what appeared to be an office, she was ready to leave.

The officer went to his car to start his watchman turn for the day. The house would still be of interest to those who might want to harm Katie. Patrick make a few calls to make sure the house would be outfitted with new, hard-to-pick deadbolt locks, front and back.

That taken care of, they headed out. She watched as her neighborhood disappeared into the background. Katie didn't ask Patrick where they were going, but she was relieved when she realized they were on the way back to his place.

"Settle in as best as you can. It's small but at least it's safe."

Katie spent 5-10 minutes unpacking the few things she needed right away but kept most of her belongings in the suitcase. Afterwards, she went back to the living room.

"Let me give you an update of what we know about the car bombing," Patrick started, "besides the confirmation of the explosives and the motives. I know it's repetitive but we always learn something from repeating our assumptions and what we think we know in this matter.

"First and foremost: Who might have been involved in the bombing, meaning not only who might have *done* it but also who might have *ordered* it. The latter is always difficult because we don't know where to look. After turning over any possibility, Patrick summarized: "Alright. My experience tells me, that the honchos don't do the dirty work themselves. They have henchmen hired to do it. You either use your own fixers or you find someone who will do the job for a high enough sum of money, and . . .”

“Where do you get guys like that?” Katie wondered out loud.

“The Dark Net, typically.

“I’ll go to Salt Lake City on Monday, and I have some ideas as to how we possibly can find that out. Then we will see what role you can play.”

“Can I go with you? I mean, for safety?” She knew it was a lame excuse, so she added, “And if I *can* play a role, it may be useful I’m there. Actually,” Katie hesitated for a moment, not sure if it was appropriate to suggest anything to the police, “how about Hannah? She’s still an insider in the Order.”

Patrick was taken back, but only for a moment. “That’s a darn good idea. Let’s see if we can get that message to Hannah and see if she even can get away.”

“She would love to. If Matthew is home it might be hard to explain without making him suspicious. If he’s gone, Hannah just has to let Isaiah know, since she works for him now.”

“I’ll use the texting system we have together . . . well, you know how it works with books in the library. I’ll ask her today.”

“Excellent.”

Patrick got up and got ready to leave the apartment. “I’ll try to be home early. I’ll cater in some dinner for us and I’ll text your burner when I leave the station. You have it with you?”

Katie patted her purse and nodded. When Patrick had left, Katie sent a brief note to Hannah’s burner:

> *Macki needs you all M - Strtng 8A.*
> *Can you go?*

A few minutes later, a response ticked in.

> *M is away, so Y.*
> *Mtng plc?*

Since Patrick would pick her up, Katie answered *SeaBisquit*, knowing Hannah would understand the meeting place was the library in Idaho Falls.

She was relieved.

CHAPTER TWENTY-THREE

KATIE AND PATRICK MET HANNAH at the library in Idaho Falls at 8:00 a.m.. Patrick stood back as he watched the two women engage in a heartwarming greeting and hugs and exclamations about "it's been soooo long."

A few minutes later, they were on their way to Salt Lake City. The conversation on the way was about everything other than the matter ahead of them. They arrived refreshed and ready for what hopefully would be a big step forward.

Linda Barnes, Jasmine White and Eddie Galway were already in the conference room when Katie, Hannah and Patrick entered. Linda, who had been informed about Katie and Hannah's attendance, welcomed them warmly and expressed the condolences of the team to Katie for the loss of her husband.

Both Katie and Hannah were fascinated by Jasmine's exotic, smooth and chocolate-colored skin and beautiful afro do. Not the typical police officer, was the initial reaction, 'but what do I know?' they both reminded themselves. 'And why not, actually?'

"We have a lot of pieces to put together," Linda started. "We ended the last meeting with 5 tasks. Why don't we take them one by one from the top and see where we are?

"Number one is the car bombing in Idaho Falls involving Bryan Carlson. Patrick, will you report?"

Patrick repeated the conclusion about the plastic explosive and that Katie had been the target. Patrick listed the people who should be further looked into as perpetrators, strongly leaning towards the idea that it was a hired job. "So, nothing new in that regard, other than Katie's protection."

"We'll get to that in a few minutes," Linda said. "Number two was the car accident in Atlanta involving Dan Hancock. Eddie?"

Eddie explained that he and the team in Atlanta agreed that the computer in Dan Hancock's car had been hacked with the purpose of causing the accident. Katie shuddered by the whole concept that someone can disable a car from a remote computer. Eddie agreed with Patrick that this, too, was a hired job and the focus will be to find people who were *there* at that moment.

"Very well," Linda continued. "Patrick, Katie and I will report on point number three," Linda said, "and now we can add Hannah as a crucial component. Thanks, Hannah for being here.

"In relation to information about transactions, we have Hannah's input that we will continue to feed to IRS who has allocated two agents from the fraud apartment. The most important thing to mention is that I have also discussed with them a plan for how catch Matthew and Nicolas in the middle of a deal. That emphasizes the importance of Hannah's input. We will discuss that plan later.

"So, Jasmine, tell us what you experienced on Cyprus."

Jasmine told the group about the meeting with the president of the largest bank on Cyprus, the meeting with a bodyguard onboard *Sirius 2*, and the scuffle that led to the disabling of him. Katie and Hannah looked at one another, shaking their heads by the mere thought of being in that situation. 'Police work is no joking matter,' Katie thought. Jasmine continued by mentioning the intercepted phone conversation between the bank president and the man onboard *Sirius 2*, which led to a conclusion about the players and how they operate.

"For the sake of keeping everyone on the same page," Linda said, "explain to us how you tapped that conversation between the bank president and Stan on *Sirius 2*."

"Well, I used a so-called IMSI grabber. That is . . ."

"A what-grabber?" Patrick asked.

"An IMSI. That requires a bit of tech talk, so bear with me.

"IMSI is a device . . . hold on. Let me show you." Jasmine dug into her purse and pulled out a small electronic devise and put it on the conference table. "This is an IMSI grabber. As you can see, it's small and discreet like a normal phone charger, and that's the point. When you put it into a power outlet, no one pays attention to it. And as the name suggests, it grabs a signal from cell phones that are being used in a conversation."

"Like a cell tower?" Patrick asked.

"Precisely! The people talking believe the conversation goes to and from their phones *via* the cell tower of the service provider, as it normally does. But, *without the participants's knowledge,* their conversation is *routed via our device* before it goes to the cell tower. But you need to be close enough to one of the persons to do that. And the Ladies Room in the Cyprus bank building was next door to the president's office. I should add that the specific IMSI I used had a battery pack in it, so I didn't need a power outlet.

"Anyway, this specific device," Jasmine tapped on the IMSI, "is called *Pwnie PhonePlug* and you can actually get it on the Internet."

"I have a question," Patrick said. "Don't you need the phone number of the person you want to hack?"

"Yes, and I had the phone number of the direct line of the bank director. Linda had gotten it to set up the meeting."

The IMSI was passed around to everyone at the table. Hannah cocked her head when she had it in her hand. "So, if I had one of these . . . Grabbers? I could listen in on Matthew's and Isaiah's phone calls?"

"That's the point we'll get to in a minute," Linda said. "So, in short, besides knocking out a guy twice your size, what did you learn that relates to this case?"

"First, I guess, Nicolas d'Aubert is really Nicolas Ionescu. Secondly, and very important, Nicolas clearly operates with a large network of people in all the areas he's engaged in. He works with the Cyprus bank director, not just doing business with him, but being informed about activities relevant to his businesses. That's how the Stan-guy on the yacht knew my name. I think we have to assume Nicolas has police officers, people in banks, customs, maybe even IRS and EPA on his payroll. Heck, maybe inside FBI? He will pay them handsomely for their loyalty, for looking the other way, and for information that keeps Nicolas out of trouble and one step ahead of the police, IRS, EPA, and whomever."

"May I comment on that?" Hannah said.

"Please do," Linda said.

"I think it's very true," Hannah started, "what Jasmine said about Nicolas's people, that is. That must be what Nicolas means when he talks to Matthew and Isaiah about his 'umbrella,'" Hannah said, fingering the quotation marks, "and that they therefore don't need to worry about IRS showing up auditing the Order, or inspections of the plant, and so on."

"Thanks, Hannah, that's very important confirmation."

"May I?" asked Katie, who had been quiet throughout the entire morning.

"Go ahead," Linda said.

"I guess it emphasizes the importance of detailed documentation about the operation," Katie said. "And this is where Hannah and I can help." Linda looked at Hannah who nodded.

"Excellent,' Linda said, "and we need that help. Then we just have to get closer to Nicolas. Before we go to the last point, what news do we have on point number four, the cover on Katie?"

Patrick mentioned that two officers will monitor Katie's house. He referred to the intrusion of her home and that Katie temporarily stayed in his apartment to protect her. He argued for why she could not check in at a hotel, motel or other facility. Hannah looked at Katie when Patrick mention her staying there, but Katie's face was unreadable.

In that sense, task number four was complete.

"Great thinking, Patrick," Linda said. "And that brings us to the last point from last meeting. Putting a tail on Nicolas, Matthew and Isaiah."

"Before we get to that," Patrick said, "I'm concerned about Hannah, to be honest. If Katie was the target of the car bomb, then someone must wonder how she—being outside the Order—gets the inside information they are afraid of being leaked. And if not Isaiah, then Hannah is the prime candidate since she works with him."

"Good point," Linda said. "Let's cover Hannah any time she's away from the premises of the Order. Do we need RF transmitters, like an ankle bracelet?" When she saw the surprise on Hannah's face, she added, "Not an ankle bracelet, per se. Just a small electronic device!"

"Hold that thought for a second," Patrick said. "I'd be careful with anything that can be traced by a suspicious person. I'd much prefer a physical shadow and protection for Hannah."

"I can see that," Linda said. "And now, to the last point: Putting a tail on Nicolas, Matthew and Isaiah. Matthew and Isaiah will be covered with the IMSI, but we probably need to have a physical tail on them as well. Do you have the resources for that, Patrick?"

"Not off-hand," Patrick said, "but I'll see if we can reorganize ourselves a little."

With that agreed, the meeting ended with a discussion about how to place an IMSI close to Nicolas.

"I'd wait with that IMSI," Eddie suggested. "We're mostly interested in conversations between Nicolas and Gooding Bioenergy. That we can cover with IMSIs in Matthew's and Isaiah's offices. I think we should focus on the hired fixers. The guys, women perhaps, who got close to Hancock and Katie. If we assume—and that maybe a wild guess—that these persons could be Nicolas's bodyguards, then the question is: How do we prove that?"

"Any ideas, yourself?" Linda asked.

"Yes, actually, but let me work on that for a few days."

"It's legal, I hope," Linda said.

"It will involve some very sophisticated hacking," Eddie said with a smile.

"OKay. Then I'll get a judge's permission to do that," Linda said and added, "to be on the safe side."

CHAPTER TWENTY-FOUR

BACK IN HIS OFFICE, EDDIE called one of his long time buddies from the high school.

"I need some information," Eddie said when Kram answered on the first ring. Kram was the backwards spelling of Mark, which Eddie always thought was a pretty plain moniker for such a sophisticated guy, but Eddie had gotten used to it—and liked it.

Kram was the top math genius in high school. He had been into computers and cyber security for years. There was literally nothing he could not hack—or get hacked. That was not a bragging statement by Kram. Eddie had learned that from a number of 'situations,' as they called them, when he had been floored by what Kram could find out. He believed Kram and his team were ahead of the police and FBI; they might even be ahead of the military.

One thing Eddie admired and respected was that Kram adhered to the unusual level of ethics of never using hacked information for his own benefit. And Kram knew that when Eddie called, it was a needy request.

"Anything, my friend. Explain."

"The name of the target is Nicolas Ionescu, Romanian by birth, but homegrown in California. He's business card reads Marquis Nicolas d'Aubert," Eddie spelled out the last name, "but he most likely operates under numerous aliases. His business is oil and biofuel and it goes under the name *Sirius*. His biggest deals are made with an Idaho company called Gooding Bioenergy. Owner there is Matthew Smith. Nicolas and Matthew are being investigated for fraud at a half a billion dollar level of public money—-yours and mine, mind you—and his bodyguards may be involved in one murder in Atlanta and another murder in Idaho Falls. The latter was a mistaken identity."

"But still a murder, right?"

"Precisely. The name of one of Nicolas's bodyguards is Stan, possibly a resident of Cyprus, where one of Nicolas's yachts, named *Sirius 2*, is moored for part of the year."

"His location?"

"Probably several places, and often his yachts. His official address is in Santa Monica." Eddie gave as many details that the *Peregrine* team had on Nicolas Ionescu, including the Gooding Bioenergy partnership.

"Time sensitive?"

"Yesterday would be perfect."

"Consider it done, buddy. We need to get together soon."

"Sure, man. As soon as this case is over with."

#

"Excellent meeting," Patrick said as Katie, Hannah, and he drove back home to Idaho. "I'm glad both of you came along. We still have a lot of work ahead of us. Are you both OK with the roles you'll play in these cases? I mean, are you comfortable with the risks associated with the roles? We are dealing with some hardcore criminals."

Both Katie and Hannah confirmed their support for the decisions made at the meeting.

It was early evening before Patrick dropped Hannah off at the Idaho Falls Library. "Sorry you have to drive back home from here after we passed right by the Order on the way, but I thought it was safer than going to your local library in Gooding," Patrick said."

"Don't think about it," Hannah said. "We'll be in contact soon. I need to get two ISMSs as soon as you have them."

"I'll have them for you tomorrow."

Hannah and Katie expressed gratitude for having been together and hugged before Hannah went to her car and drove off. Katie and Patrick only had a few more minutes before they were back at his apartment.

CHAPTER TWENTY-FIVE

MATTHEW WAS IN ISTANBUL WITH Nicolas. They planned real estate investments in Turkey, Greece and Cyprus, "Places where nosy people don't look," Nicolas said, "and we need to park some of the G99 profit in real estate. Safest place for having it later in life. Like a few years from now," he said with a smirk, "when we are tired of running around in the world."

They visited a dozen places, everything from bare land and land prepared for development, to condos and sports centers. Nicolas had a dream of building a vacation center. He already had a name for it. Matthew didn't have to ask what it was. They purchased land and buildings for more than hundred million dollars, facilitated by the Ziraat Bankasi bank in Ankara.

The president and the chief lending officer followed them everywhere. At lunch, they took Nicolas and Matthew to Rotary meetings and private golf clubs, and at night they took them to famous and not so famous night clubs. They were treated like royalties everywhere. Matthew learned to appreciate the culinary treats of the Middle Eastern cuisine, although he still preferred Budweiser over the local wines. In his opinon *ouzo* shouldn't even be called wine.

At the last meeting with Ziraat Bankasi in Ankara, Nicolas brought up the subject that had motivated their trip to the country.

"We have some payment problems with a large customer here in Turkey and we could use some help." The Ziraat president nodded, but looked less committed than Nicolas had hoped, so he squeezed the thumb screws a bit. "We can have it done in Nicosia, where we are going after this trip, but I'd rather do it in the country of the customer," Nicolas said.

"Oh, don't worry, we'll take care of your needs. Let me hear the details."

"Thank you, Erdem." They were not on first name basis, but Nicolas wanted to sound friendly and close. "Here's the situation." Nicolas explained that a large order for B99 had been placed by a midsized oil distributor near Istanbul. He owns a number of gas stations and . . ."

"We're familiar with all of them," Erdem said.

"Good. Well, our problem is that we have already shipped the product, worth twenty-five million U.S. dollars from Matthew's factory to Istanbul. The customer paid the upfront five million dollars fee but he has cash flow problems with the rest. We would like you to extend a line of credit to him of twenty-to-twenty-five million dollars, collateralized by the cargo—Matthew pushed the documents across the table—after it arrives in Istanbul in two weeks."

Erdem hesitated. It was a much larger deal than they usually made for a single transaction, but he looked over the paperwork . . . and agreed. Before he could ask the question, Nicolas added, "You will of course get a five percent fee for the service."

"Very good. We have a deal," Erdem said and offered his hand. The three men shook hands simultaneously.

#

After a week in Turkey, Nicolas and Matthew flew to Cyprus and were picked up in the airport by a driver from Republic Bank of Cyprus. Instead of going to Nicosia, they drove to Lanarca to have a meeting on *Sirius 2*. When they arrived, bank president K. Demetriou—he liked to go by his first initial rather than his first name—was already sitting on the stern sun deck with a glass of Chablis in his hand.

"Welcome," Nicolas said as they boarded and nodded in the direction of Stan, "glad you've been taken care of already."

"Your staff is impeccable," Demetriou said.

"They are paid well to be that way," Nicolas answered with pride. "This is Matthew, my primary partner in the USA," Nicolas said, bringing Matthew into the conversation. The two men shook hands.

"I should have arrived a few days ago," Demetriou said with a smile."I could get used to this place."

"I've told you many times that *Sirius 2* is always available to you and your wife.

"Shall we?" Nicolas gestured towards a large table in the shade. They sat down and started their business. As Stan brought ice tea to the table, Nicolas noticed his limp.

"What the heck is wrong with you, Stan?"

"I fell down the stairs several weeks ago and tore the ACL in my right knee. It's better now."

"What? Can you not . . .?"

"I rushed myself for no real reason, so it was a slip. I was barefooted."

"Geez, I may have to reduce your salary if you are not one-hundred percent," Nicolas joked. "Anyway, gentlemen," Nicolas said in an upbeat tone, "we want to look at properties in Limassol, perhaps enough to create a small amusement park. Hotels with swimming pools and a few mini golf courses are not enough for the tourists any more. New tourists are important, but getting previous customers to *return* requires new tricks. We need some Universal Studio-type rides and entertainment. And we want Republic Bank of Cyprus to handle the finances." We will forward twenty-five million dollars to you in two weeks so you can secure the land for our project." After a long conversation about Nicolas's dream project, they summed things up.

"We'll be happy to do so. It's always both fun, creative, and lucrative to do business with you, so we're in on that deal."

"Excellent. And the fee will be attractive."

"Generous as usual," Demetriou said.

#

On the way back to Houston, where Nicolas and Matthew were going to split up, they discussed some more deals. Nicolas had received an 'able, willing, and ready' request from a customer they had not done business with in a long time. He was in Panama, which, despite it's proximity to U.S.A., was a new market for the Sirius and Gooding Bioenergy.

"Let's look at that when we have settled in and taken stock of what's going on elsewhere," Matthew. "Maybe Ron Patterson can do some scouting there for us," he added.

Nicolas like that idea. "Certainly," he said.

They exchanged a manly hug and thanked themselves for a great trip, wished themselves good luck with their future business, and split up.

Matthew was in high spirit when he finally arrived in Magic Valley, Twin Falls airport where Isaiah waited. As the two brothers drove home to the Order, Matthew expressed the need for a private jet. "Waiting for commercial planes in every airport is a waste of time. Nicolas never does that."

"C'mon, Matt. Don't you have enough toys? You're becoming a copy of Nicolas, even in your clothing and shoes, and if I'm not mistaken, his cologne, too."

"You already said that. I see nothing wrong with copying success, do you?"

"Business-wise, no! But at the personal level, yes. I'm not so sure your wives want to be married to a copy of Nicolas."

"She's in her own world. I don't think she enjoys my company and I don't enjoy hers, either, to be honest. Thanks goodness for multiple wives. But back to a private jet . . ."

"Neither one of us can fly an airplane, for crying out loud. Let's keep the . . ."

"We'll get a pilot, of course," Matthew tried.

"I'd say no. Let's keep the money in the business. If it keeps growing as it has in the past several years, we need a larger plant, or even a third plant."

"Hmm. Well, you may be right about that, Isaiah," Matthew said, thinking about the new big deals on the horizon.

CHAPTER TWENTY-SIX

PATRICK, KATIE, AND HANNAH MET Eddie Galway in a separate meeting in Twin Falls at the Koto Brewing Company, one of Patrick's favorite local outlets for handcrafted beer. It was close to the airport and not too far from where he and Katie lived.

Since the two car accidents were now officially declared criminal cases, the only subject for the two detectives was to determine how they might be able to get close to the perpetrators.

"Like I said at the last meeting in Salt Lake," Eddie started, "I have an idea. A friend of mine works with quite a large group of people who, eh, I guess the best way to put it is: Hack computers and phones. Unbeknownst to almost all smart phone owners, the internal GPS app on our phones keeps a historic record of where you have been in the past, at least within a certain amount of time.

"We all know GPS follows us when we move around—that's why we can use it in traffic—but we typically *don't* look at our own GPS records because we don't need to check where we have been . . . since *we* were there ourselves. Follow me?" They all nodded.

"So, to see what that requires, follow me now on your own phone, OK? Go to *Settings*, then *Privacy*. Find *Location Services* and open a folder called *Significant Locations*. You need a password to open that folder, of course. So, enter that." Eddie sat back while each one of them followed his instructions.

"What do you see? A lot of places, right? Check on Wednesday last week. Where were you at 12:30 p.m.?"

"Central part of Salt Lake City," Katie said.

"Same here, "Hannah said.

"And you, Patrick?"

"Same place," he answered. "And it even gives you the exact

geographical coordinates. Wow!"

"Good. Check out on your map, what was there at those coordinates."

"Patrick looked at his map. "FBI head quarters! Wow."

"Yes, indeed. And my phone says the same," Eddie said. "That's because all of us were at the exact same place: In a meeting with Linda."

"But if we want to do that kind of spying on another person's phone we need to get to that phone, right?" Patrick asked.

"Correct!" Eddie said. "But we can find ways to overcome that."

"But we don't know the perpetrators, do we?" Katie asked.

"Not yet," Eddie said, "but let's make an assumption here: The perpetrator is most likely one or more of Nicolas's fixers or bodyguards—assuming Matthew and Isaiah don't have such people?" Hannah shook her head. "Good, so we need to be very creative in order to get access to their phones."

"Well, I can get Matthew's phone at any time and Isaiah's is easy, too, since I work in his office," Hannah said.

"Great. I hoped you'd say that," Eddie said and looked at Hannah a with a smile. "Now, how about Nicolas?" There was silence.

"If your friend, or friend's friends," Hannah started probingly, "can hack any given smart phone, can the hacker then also get access to the phone register, I mean, to the person's contact list?"

"Good question, Hannah. I'm pretty sure the answer is yes, but I'll confirm that with Kram."

"If that's the case, I can get Nicolas's phone number from Matthew's or Esaiah's phone," Hannah continued. "And from Nicolas's phone we should be able to get phone numbers of all his contacts. But from what I understand, Nicolas has a huge number of contacts; so it would be a monster job to . . ."

"Wait," Katie said. "Maybe not. I'd imagine Nicolas has the phone numbers of his fixers on speed dial—because he needs them all the time—if that's true, then it would be only a small group out of his entire contact list. Maybe five or ten?"

"Wow, Katie," Eddie sat back for a moment. "You're on top of things in cyber word."

"I'm learning from listening to you guys," Katie said with a smile, sending a wink in Patrick's direction.

"Great. So, when Hannah gets Mathew's phone we're on our way. And it would be logical to assume the fixers were right at or near the crime scenes on the two specific dates, which are, to repeat ourselves, January 20 and February 14 of this year. All clear on that?"

Everyone confirmed those days.

"Anything else?" Eddie asked.

"I need one of those grabbers," Hannah said.

"Right. Thanks for reminding me. I almost forgot," Eddie said. "Linda got six Pwnie PhonePlugs like the one Jasmine showed at the meeting. I have four of them in my car and I already have one myself."

"If anyone needs the last one, let me know," Eddie added.

"Let me have one extra for Isaiah's office," Hannah said. "Since it's in the other end of the office building."

When they broke up, they went to the parking lot where Hannah, Katie, and Patrick each got their Pwnies.

#

Back in the office, Hannah looked for power outlets for the two Pwnie units. She wanted them to be inconspicuous, so they wouldn't be removed by someone who accidentally would come across them. The twin plug behind the big office printer in Isaiah's office was ideal, in Hannah's opinion, as was the plug behind the couch in Matthew's office. 'That should also be close enough for covering the conference room next door.

After inserting them, Hannah crossed her fingers that it would work out.

CHAPTER TWENTY-SEVEN

THE FOLLOWING WEEK WAS THE start of the school's summer vacation in 2014 and the offices at Gooding Biofuel were pretty much empty of people.

That was an ideal opportunity for Hannah to copy the documents of the last ten deals Gooding Bioenergy had made.

A large one was to Istanbul and the first shipment was already underway. She was aware of that deal from listening to conversations about it between Matthew and Isaiah. It was a deal twice as large as the botched Indian deal a few years ago.

'So far so good,' Hannah thought. 'We shall see what the tax credit statement shows.'

When the shipment arrived in the port of Istanbul, Matthew discussed with Isaiah what the documents to EPA for B99 should be made out to be. Matthew called Nicolas and they agreed on 2.5 million barrels shipped in an LR2 carrier. Papers were worked out to show that.

'So,' Hannah thought, 'they sell 1.3 million gallons and charge the customer for that; and he gets it; so, *he's* satisfied. But they claim tax credits for a 2.5 million gallons based on 'authentic documents.'

She sat back, stunned by the discrepancy.

'That's millions of dollars credit on top of the profit from the actual B99 supply.' She was in disbelief. 'Oh my God!'

Hannah had both the documents for the shipment and for the EPA application. And the IMSI had recorded Matthew's and Isaiah's many conversations about the deal.

Hannah also had plenty of time to go through the contact list on Matthew's phone. Nicolas's two phone numbers were not hard to find.

She made a note of them and texted Katie on their second burner:

Next book in the series is out on 14th.
Does Macki want it? 10A

A few minutes later a text came back with:
Yes, Macki wants it.
C U

The next day, Hannah, Katie and Patrick met at 10 a.m. in the library. Patrick was excited about the papers Hannah brought with her but even more excited about having Matthew's phone list. "I'll share that with Eddie as soon as we break up here. He'll get back to us really soon," he said.

#

Kram called Eddie the same evening.

"That wasn't too hard. Give me some challenging stuff next time, will you?" He chuckled.

"First of all, neither Matthew nor Isaiah were on the two crime scenes on the dates we are looking at. And neither was Nicolas.

"Second, I got a list of Nicolas's contacts and phone number, most of the addresses, etc. . . . oh, by the way, one of them was the Stan-man you mentioned . . . Man, that Nicolas-guy has a lot of connections. Anyway, a lot of them I could eliminate, assuming the likes of Nicolas's hair dresser or the lawn and aquarium guys aren't key players in your mystery." He chuckled again. "About a dozen had potential to be 'fixers' as you called them, due to . . . well, that's not important. I ran a profile on all of them through their phone bills and addresses. I got their credit card numbers, etc."

"How about hacking their . . .?"

"Patience, buddy, patience. I'm getting there. I have to make it sound like it was complicated, otherwise you won't thank me *profusely* afterwards.

"So, out of the dozen or so candidates, one person, but not the Stan-man, was in Idaho Falls the day Bryan Carlson was killed. That is evidenced by the GPS history. On top of it, his credit card showed he flew in from Coeur d'Alene in Idaho—too lazy to drive, I guess—and checked in at Motel 8 on I-15 the night before. The day after, he left the area with the 1:05 p.m. flight back home. His GPS does not indicate he visited any *other* areas in Idaho than this specific one. I would call it 'a definite suspect.'

"What's his name?" Eddie asked.

"Darn! I forgot to check that?"

"You what? How can . . ." Kram's laughter brought Eddie back from his shock. "OK! Let me have it."

"Kenny Brown."

"Awesome. Thanks so much," Eddie said. "I'll get back to you la . . ."

"Hey, wait! I'm not done yet. Don't you want to hear about the guy in Atlanta?"

"Oh, yes, of course. I was so excited that I forgot about . . ."

"Sorry, pal. But there was no guy."

Eddies hearts sank, but the brewing laughter made Eddie realize Kram was pulling his leg.

"OK, what's her name? He wondered what might be coming. With Kram one never knew.

"Correct guess. It was a *woman*. Jane Easton is her name. She was in contact with Nicolas several times the days before and on the 20th of January. She lives in Union City, south-west of Atlanta—delightfully close to Hartfield international airport, by the way—so she didn't have to book a hotel or an airplane ticket to be at the car crash location.

"I have a very precise GPS coordinate from her phone. It literally matches a sharp right curve of the eastbound Fulton Parkway after you get out of Chattahoochie Hill. He might have been in Chattahoochee that day and was heading home to south-Atlanta through the wooded area. How Jane knew Hancock would be on *that* road at *that* time is up to you guys to figure out. Given the time of the accident, she might not have worked alone, but I have no data from my research to back that up. I would call her 'a definite suspect,' too."

"I thank you, Kram. *Profusely!*" Eddie said, laughing. "That must have been quite a complicated matter." After a few minutes of small talk, they hung up.

#

Eddie immediately arranged a phone conference with Linda and Patrick.

"So, Linda, we need two things. I need permission to hack the phones of Nicolas, Jane Easton and Kenny Brown and put spyware on all three of them," Eddie said. "We have pretty strong indications that

Jane and Kenny are fixers for Nicolas and were involved in the car murder of Hancock and the murder attempt on Katie, respectively. At least, their GPS coordinates for the locations on the specific dates and times match completely with the accidents."

"How did you . . .?"

"The 'super-techies.' They knows those things; I don't do things like that, for obvious reasons." Linda nodded her accept although Eddie couldn't see that.

"The other thing is: We are now at a tipping point where *we* can control the information flow *and* prompt specific activities. I'd like to start with this: Let's have the Chief of Police in Boise and Atlanta notify the newspapers in the two states that there has been some progress in the respective cases and that the police are closing in on a couple of suspects. That'll get some people jumping in their seats and start some intense phone conversations or texting between them right after."

"Sounds quite likely," Linda said. "I like that! I'll call both police departments after we break up here and ask them to put out the announcements tomorrow. Out of curiosity, what spyware will your friend use?"

"He will most likely use a new, secret Israeli spyware program called *Pegasus*. That software can *without a trace* infect a smartphone and allow users—in this case, you, me, Patrick or others—to download every bit of data from a phone while also monitoring key strokes, watching through the phone camera, and even listening through a microphone—even when the phone is off! And even with the battery taken out of the phone."

"Jeez! How come I don't know something like that?"

"Well, it's very new and only used at national security levels. CIA and the military may have it, but I agree, FBI need to have it, too. Anyway . . . I think this will be an important step in . . ."

"But what if they use burner phones?" Patrick interjected.

"I was going to ask the same question," Linda said.

"In that case, we'll have to rely on the IMSI recordings. Having both will tighten the rope around them."

"Good. Consider it done," Linda said.

CHAPTER TWENTY-EIGHT

THE NEXT DAY, MATTHEW WAS pulled off of the rosy cloud he'd been on because of a string of recent, successful deals.

"What the Hell is going on?" Nicolas screamed.

"You need to be more specific," Matthew said unaffected, getting used to Nicolas's temper tantrums. "What's going on here right now is that we're getting ready for a grill party, and . . ."

"Fuck your party. Someone is giving the police some information that helps them closing in on two cases, and I think . . ."

"Which cases are we talking about. The Istanbul deal was as clean as anything we have ever . . ."

"I'm talking about the car accident with Hancock and the blow-up of the car with the husband of your former Order member, whatever her name was. The pretty, young girl that ran away with . . ."

"Katie?"

"Katie, yes!"

"Are you telling me you *knew* about these cases? Is that what you meant when you told me Hancock was no longer in the business? That is was not an accident but a crime? Are you fucking crazy?"

"Watch your mouth, Matt."

"One more question before I hang up." Matthew knew the answer but wanted to hear it from Nicolas.

"You just said 'Someone is giving the police information that helps them closing in on two cases, and I think . . .' Those were your words. What exactly were you thinking?"

"I think your Order is leaking information to or collaborating with the police, that's what I think. It could be anyone as far as I'm concerned. It could even be you."

"And why on Earth would I do that?"

"I have no idea. But weirder things have happened."
Matthew hung up.

#

Two hundred miles away, Eddie smiled and texted Patrick and Linda: "Got them. More to come."

#

"How's Katie these days?" Matthew asked Hannah over dinner.

"Katie Carlson?"

"Katie Smith," Matthew corrected.

"Well, if we're talking about the same Katie, her name is Katie Carlson. She got married. That's why she left the Order. To get married to someone of her choice." Hannah didn't volunteer any other information.

"But . . . she never . . ."

"She got married, OK?"

"OK. So, how's she doing?"

"As of right now? I have no idea. I haven't talked with her in ages. Last time, I think it was shortly after she got married, she had a job of her choice, was happy and bubbly, had a successful husband, and enjoyed freedom."

"Is that what you call life outside the Order? Freedom?"

"That's what *she* called it," Hannah said tersely.

"You know her husband got killed? His car blew up."

"Yes, I heard it on TV a couple of days after it happened and I read about it in the Idaho Falls Daily News. It must've been devastating. She has not been in contact with anyone since—that *I* know of at least. I asked Isaiah if they have been in contact but he hasn't heard a thing either. Understandably, in my view. It will take some time to get over. A long time, I would imagine. Why are you suddenly interested in . . .?"

"The two of you were quite close, I think."

"That doesn't answer my question. But, yes, I liked her a lot."

"Someone mentioned her name today," Matthew said matter-of-factly.

"Is that so? Then why don't you ask that 'someone' what he or she knows about Katie."

#

"Are you reading the newspapers every day? Watching the news?" Nicolas asked when he called Jane Easton.

"What kind of question is that? Of course I do. Why?"

"If you ask why, you're not reading or watching the news."

"What news are we talking about, Nick. The Atlanta Braves just won the . . . Never mind. You need to be more specific, otherwise . . ."

"The police in Atlanta talk about a suspect in the car accident that you . . . shall we say, helped with?"

"They have nothing that points to me, I can assure you that. That was a clean strike."

"I'm glad to hear that, but you know what? I'd like you to go on a trip to Cyprus. You need a vacation for a week or two. I have a ticket ready for you at the Turkish Airlines ticket counter in Hartsfield. For Wednesday at 8:20 p.m.."

"Day after tomorrow?"

"Of course. Why wait?"

"I can't."

"You can if I tell you to."

"Not at all. It's a medical reason. I cannot fly for another 6 days."

"What's the . . .?"

"None of your business," Jane said firmly. "I can fly a week from now. But I can move in with my sister for a few days if you think that's a . . ."

"Good idea. So, just change your ticket with Turkish Airlines and you're fine. Stan will be onboard *Sirius 2* when you get there."

"I don't want to be alone on *Sirius 2* with Stan. All he wants is to get into my panties."

"I would, too. It's been a long . . . Well, bring a girlfriend."

"No, he'll just want to get into her panties, too."

"Never mind. Pack up and go next week. Text me when you have changed the ticket. I'll be over there myself shortly."

#

It was only 4:30 in the morning when Kenny Brown's phone woke him up. He looked at the digital clock on the bed stand.

"Who the Hell calls at this . . . " he said to himself, sleep drunk and irritated. When he saw it was Nicolas, he answered. "Good morning." Kenny tried to sound upbeat. "Good hearing from you."

Without any prelude, Nicolas jumped right into the reason for his call. "The police in Idaho think they have the guy who blew up Bryan Carlson's car a couple of months ago."

"I'm glad to hear that. They have nothing on me. So, let's hope the guy is in jail already and the case is closed."

"You sound pretty confident?"

"Absolutely. There's no trace of me. I read they found residues of the plastic explosive on the wreckage, but anyone can get that on the Internet."

"Is that how you got it?"

"I wasn't born yesterday, Nick. Shopping on the Internet leaves a trail. No, I got it through my personal network. Not traceable."

"Well, let hope it stays that way."

#

Six hundred miles away, Eddie smiled and texted Patrick and Linda: "Two for two."

#

When Eddie had Kram's information about the re-booking of Jane Easton's flight, Jasmine booked a flight to Cyprus on the same airline and asked for a seat next to Easton.

"That seat is already booked, Ma'am. But I can . . ."

"Change it!"

"I cannot do . . ."

"Change it! This is a request by FBI. I can give you my badge ID or put my boss on the line if that . . ."

"Eh, hold on a sec." A moment later, the reservation clerk confirmed the wanted seat.

"And no traveler in the third seat in that row, OK?"

"Eh, yes, Ma'am."

#

After a quick trip to FBI's headquarters in Washington DC, where Linda outlined the plan for catching Nicolas and Matthew red-handed, she was back in the Salt Lake City. She had gotten full global support by both FBI and Interpol for the *Peregrine* project in whatever city or country it may be needed.

Now, she called the five 'peregrines' together on a ZOOM conference. She spent an hour outlining the plan she and FBI in Washington had devised with IRS and EPA. It was as brilliant as it was simple, but every link in the chain had to perform 100%. Backup could be difficult.

For another hour, questions were raised, problems were tossed around, 'what-if' scenarios were debated, but in the end, the plan was as watertight as it could be.

After a thorough outlining of the role of each of the individuals, Linda sat back with a sense of accomplishment, although she admitted to herself that she hadn't really accomplished anything until the plan was successfully executed.

CHAPTER TWENTY-NINE

BY THE TIME THE TURKISH Airlines flight to Nicosia made a two hour stopover in Athens, Jane Easton and Jasmine White had gotten to know one another well. As they learned about the other's travel plans, they found it an amusing coincidence that they were both continuing from Athens to Nicosia. They laughed, discussed, and shared experiences about traveling abroad as single women and doing business in a male dominated world. They even shared little ideas about how to make that more safe.

Jane was a medical sales rep for J&J, covering all of Georgia from her home office outside Atlanta. That gave her time to engage in other things like sports, being in a book club, and go out with friends. She loved the idea of Jasmine's free lance writing job, and found it fascinating that she was writing about the history of the Green Line on Cyprus.

"I've only been to Cyprus as a tourist. I love the beaches of Limassol," Jane told Jasmine. "If you have time, you absolutely must go there. A colleague of mine has a boat on the south coast. That's where I'm headed this time."

Jane and Jasmine did not have seats together on the flight to Nicosia, so they decided to meet in the arrival hall after going through immigration and getting their luggage—and before Jane would drive to the South coast while Jasmine would stay overnight in Nicosia.

Despite the 22 hours flight with barely any sleep, Jane and Jasmine were surprisingly fresh. They found a Starbucks where they could have a cup of coffee in a quiet corner. As they sat down, Jane pulled a small, soft bag and a book out of her suitcase. She put the bag in the pocket of her jacket and the book on the table.

Their conversation was as lively as on the plane, but Jane noticed a couple of times that Jasmine looked past her at something in the background. 'Didn't she just nod at someone?' Jane thought.

"Someone you know?" she asked after turning her head, spotting a plainly clad man leaning against the wall, reading a magazine.

"Well, for a moment I thought so," Jasmine said calmly, "but I don't think that's the case. Wouldn't that be kind of amazing, though? I mean, being ten-thousand miles away from home and run into someone you know?" Jane agreed and laughed.

After more small talk Jasmine stunned Jane with one simple question.

"So, tell me . . . what exactly *are* you doing for Mr. Nicolas Ionesco? Is he in the medical business, too?"

Jane was stunned. She was lost for words and fear immediately showed in her eyes.

"I don't know anyone by that name," she almost studdered.

"How about Nicolas d'Aubert? Does that help?"

"I don't know anyone by that name either," Jane insisted.

"Really? I have a recording of a conversation between you and Nicolas last week where you talked about a car accident southwest of Atlanta that you called 'a clean strike,'" Jasmine said laconically. "I have it right here if you don't remember what you said."

"I've no idea of what you're talking about." Jane fidgetted in her seat, contemplating if she should get up and leave. Before she could do that, Jasmine pressed on.

"Well, then let me play it for you then." Jasmine made a few keystrokes on her phone and Jane's phone rang after a few seconds. Jane glanced at the screen but ignored it.

"That's me calling," Jasmine said. "I used that number for recording your conversation with Nicolas." Jasmine put her phone out on the table and pressed the Play button. Jane heard her own voice. In her rage and fear, Jane didn't notice the plain-clothed man had taken several steps forward and now was right behind her.

"Who the Hell are you?" Jane hissed at Jasmine while slowly reaching for the little bag in her jacket. Jasmine knew what was coming. Just as a slim hand gun came out and was pointed directly at Jasmine, the man behind her took one more step forward and delivered a crushing blow with his nightstick directly on Jane's wrist.

Jane screamed and crumbled in pain in the chair, dropping the gun, and holding her arm for protection. Jasmine got up and presented her badge. "FBI! You are under arrest for the murder of Dan Hancock.

Follow this man. He'll read your rights and take you to a place where you can stay in Athens until we decide when you can go back to Atlanta. Have a good night."

Jasmine turned to the man. "Thanks, Jim. Excellent execution. Make sure Jane has no person-to-person contact with anyone whatsoever. Not even a lawyer, which she may demand. She can keep her phone, of course." Jim knew why that was and nodded. "Very well, ma'am."

"And stay with her every moment until you both are in Athens. Linda will give you further instructions then."

"Roger that. Talk to you tomorrow," Jim said, as he put handcuffs on Jane and picked up her gun. She struggled to get onto her feet when Jim pulled her up. With pain and fury showing in her eyes, she shot Jasmine a murderous look.

"Don't forget your book," Jasmine said coldly.

That night, Jasmine sent a brief report back to Linda.

> *All steps completed successfully. Jane is safely in*
> *the 'care' of Jim. Heading out tomorrow morning*
> *for the next assignment.*
> *Jasmine.*

The next morning, Jasmine went to Istanbul, awaiting further instruction from Linda on her mission there.

#

"Nick, where's the babe?" Stan asked when he called Nicolas.

"What d'you mean?"

"Jane arrived in Nicosia Airport four hours ago and went through Immigration and cust . . ."

"Are you sure?" Nicolas asked.

"Yes, Sir. We have that confirmed by one of our people in Bagage Claim. As she was supposed to go directly to Lanarca, I thought it was a matter of two hours before she would be here on *Sirius 2*. But she's not here. And our people don't know where she is. She did not pick up her rental car."

"What's going on, Stan?"

"Have no idea."

"Well, let's not lose our cool. Find her. I'll call you tomorrow."

Nicolas sat pensively after hanging up. Had Jane decided not to go to Lanarca after arriving in Nicosia? She did have some serious hesitations about going, but she has always been dependable. Why would she change the agreed plan? Run away? What would have caused that? Cold feet after the announcement in the papers? She was so certain nothing would connect her to the Hancock accident. Could that have changed? In that case, what would that be?' He sighed. 'Dang. Too few answers.' He had to wait until he would talk with Stan tomorrow.

When Nicolas called the next day, he immediately picked up on the concern in Stan's voice.

"She was arrested by the police in the arrival hall while . . ."

"What?" Nicolas screamed. "When did, how's . . .? I mean . . ."

"Well, all we know from our contacts in the airport is that she apparently had finished having coffee with a woman—most likely another a traveler, we don't know—when someone literally grabbed her and arrested her."

"Jesus Christ, Stan, are you loosing control over things?"

"Absolutely not. We had no indication from anyone in our network that something like this *could* happen. Has Jane done something recently that has attracted the attention of the police?"

"Not to my knowledge," Nicolas lied. "Find out if this was the American, Cypriot, Greek, or Turkish police. ASAP! There must be a leak somewhere in the system. Find out who the coffee-woman was. Where's Jane now, by the way?"

"She disappeared. We have no idea who that coffee-woman was. Our focus was on Jane, and we saw her being pulled into a secluded area in the airport by an un-uniformed man."

"Check all such areas."

"Are you sure 'bout that, Nic? We're talking about walking into police custody areas. Who would I claim to be and what would I tell them as a reason for asking about Jane's whereabouts—a potential police suspect?"

"Hmm. Well. I guess that's your call. But keep me updated. Call me every day."

"Will do."

CHAPTER THIRTY

NICOLAS WAS IN A FOUL MOOD.

Nothing in his luxurious life in Santa Monica gave him any satisfaction.

There were more and more signs around him that information about his business and his people was getting out—and what was worse: Into the wrong hands.

The mood took another dive when Stan called.

"Jane is out of the country. When we finally connected with our airport people, they informed us that she had left on the morning plane to Athens with a guy. We don't know who *he* is. Police would be my guess. Whether she goes from there to Atlanta or somewhere else, we have no idea. Nor when it may happen, "

"Stan! For crying out loud. Call the airlines and ask if your sister made it onboard the plane this morning. Or . . ."

"No one in the airline is allowed to disclose that, of course—for security reasons."

"Well, then find someone who can hack the passenger lists of the airline and find out where she went afterwards."

"If she went anywhere at all," Stan ventured as a challenge. "She may still be here."

"Find that out, too, damn it." Nicolas hung up.

Stan did not want another conversation with Nicolas on a day when he was in a combative mood, so when he got additional information, he sent a laconic text message about Jane's whereabouts and Interpol's involvement.

Nicolas was on the way out of the door to go to the marina, hoping a day on the ocean aboard *Sirius* would pick up his mood. But things went from bad to worse when another text came in on his screen. It was from Kenny Brown in Idaho:

I'm in police custody. Arrested for murder.
How is that even possible?
Still have my phone so I can contact my attorney.
Probably the last message for some days.
K.

Nicolas slammed his hand on his desk and hurled his phone against the wall.

"This has to stop!" he cried out loud. He violently pushed his chair back from the desk, went to the garage, got into his Lamborghini, and sped to the Santa Monica beach. Very few people were out that morning since the weather station forecasted "inclement and rapidly deteriorating weather." That suited Nicolas just fine, but instead of a boat ride he decided to go for a brisk walk. When he got back an hour later, cold but not wet, he went into his office and called one of his bodyguards in for a briefing.

"Bruce. We have a problem in Idaho. Kenny—you know Kenny in Coeur d'Alene, right? He has been arrested. I have no idea what for," Nicolas lied. "He was supposed to keep an eye on a few members of the Toponis Order. I want you to go there and take over that assignment. Today."

Bruce Warner was one of Nicolas's bodyguards who also had a part time job at the Santa Monica Police Department where he often was referred to as 'Hawkeye.' He nodded and waited for more instructions.

"I'll have one of our pilots take you there in one hour. Private traveling is always good." Bruce nodded. "I will text your instructions when you confirm you have arrived."

"Very good," Bruce said tersely. "I'll go home and pack and be ready in 30 min."

"Perfect. And to answer the question you haven't asked yet: I don't know exactly how long you will be there, a few days, a week, or whatever. Depends on the outcome of your assignment."

"Anything you say, boss. I'm ready," Bruce confirmed. He knew he could book himself into a comfortable place, since 'money's not an issue,' as Nicolas always said.

Forty minutes later, the Cessna Citation Longitude took off, and Bruce Hawkeye settled in with a book for the next couple of hours.

Back from the airport, Nicolas drove to the beach again. With a cool, logical mind he wanted to take stock of the information he had gotten in the past months and in particular the past two-three days. The weather was not bad at all, and Nicolas felt refreshed in the strong wind.

'Who's the leak? It's gotta be someone from the Order but it would be unimaginable if it were Matt. So, who's the most obvious? I was always so sure it was the little babe, Katie. According to Matt, she was a trouble-maker since she was a kid. Didn't want to follow rules and instructions. Opposed plans . . . Well forget that damn brat. But . . . she *could* have taken a lot of information from Isaiah's office when she was there and gone to the police or whomever. But she hasn't been around the Order for a long time, and certainly not when the latest developments with Jane and Kenny have unfolded. No, I don't think she's the most likely candidate,' he concluded.

'Isaiah might be more inclined. Matt has often talked about Isaiah's concerns about the magnitude of the fraud, pointing to the risk that it would eventually attract too much attention. Good point, but on the other hand, he has gone along with everything until now.

'Who else could it be? Rita, his mother? I know so little about her. She's always in the background and that can be dangerous. Easy to overlook, therefore easy to dismiss. Nah, not likely but not one I would exclude either.

'Well, there sure are a lot of unknowns.'

On his way home, Nicolas cruised ever so slowly through the streets of Santa Monica. 'I'm overlooking something,' he thought, drumming his fingers restlessly on the steering wheel. As he got to the driveway of his house and was about to leave the car outside the garage, it struck him who was the mole.

CHAPTER THIRTY-ONE

NICOLAS SAT IN THE CAR for ten minutes contemplating the situation. He was sure now and texted Hawkeye:

Put a tail on Hannah Smith - wife of Matthew.
Follow her every move.
Put a tracer on her car. Report what you find.
You may want a few more sticks of plastic explosives.
Don't fail.
Nd'A

#

Two hundred miles away, Eddie frowned but smiled and texted Patrick and Linda.

#

Patrick asked Katie to ask Hannah to come to the little library in Gooding. Urgently—if at all possible.

Patrick and Katie were there when Hannah arrived. Patrick didn't notice any tell-tale signs of a shadow nearby her, and that was positive. He went straight to the main point.

"Eddie has obtained information from Kram to the effect that one of Nicolas's fixers, Bruce Warner—if that's his real name—is in our neighborhood searching for you, Hannah. Bruce is an employee of the police in Santa Monica—officially at least. We have learned he's often referred to as 'Hawkeye.' It could be his actual moniker but could, perhaps, also be a cover.

"We have to work from the assumptions that he's here to silence you. Therefore, we need to maintaing the constant surveillance on both you and Katie around the clock.

"Katie can stay in my place for a while longer but we'll need a place for you, too, Hannah. I'll find one.

"Questions?"

Katie shook her head but Hannah turned the situation over in her head. "Where would I be? I still go to work at the Order, away from my home."

"I'll get a place for the three of us. It would be ideal if you could be away from home for, say a week until we get a feel for the situation. Is there any chance you could take a vacation and disappear for a week or longer?"

"I don't know." She contemplated some options and said, "I could air the idea to Matthew that I'd love to go to a literature conference in San Francisco next week."

"That would be great. And soon is key," Patrick added. Hannah nodded her consent.

While they had lunch, Eddie called Patrick.

"Bruce Warner flew in to Idaho Falls on Nicolas's private plane last night. The airport log confirmed that the tail ID-number corresponds to Nicolas's Cessna."

"D'you have Bruce's location here?" Patrick asked.

"A motel not too far from the Order's compound. He used a credit card for the deposit when he checked in. Proves he's a Dumbo. We have hacked his credit card, of course, so that's confirmed. Rented an AVIS car. Credit card again. Proves he's a *stupid* Dumbo.

"I'll send the license plate number and the motel address as soon as I get it from Kram, probably in minutes. Bruce may use a burner phone although he didn't do that yesterday."

"Perfect," Patrick said.

"Put a GPS-transmitter on the car when you get close enough. We need to know where Bruce is all the time - in real time."

"Roger that!"

#

The nest morning, Bruce texted Nicolas:
>Installed near the Order.
>Spent this morning there.

No signs of Hannah.
Her car is there, though.
No phone calls we can trace.
Hawkeye

#

Eddie walked into Linda's office.

"Just the latest updates, although you have some of the pieces already," Eddie started.

"One: As you know, we have Kenny Brown in jail in Boise and Jane Easton in jail in Athens—Jasmine thought it might be best not to send her back to Atlanta just yet. As expected, we have shaken up Nicolas.

"Both Jasmine and Patrick have made sure Kenny and Jane still have their phones. We have their numbers and have a Pegasus spyware on both of them, so we want them to use their phones. And since they both are in jail, they cannot go out and get burner phones, so with Nicolas being careless, we have an ear on their doings all the time.

"Two: We're chasing one of Nicolas's fixers who arrived in Idaho last night to chase Hannah. I'll keep you updated daily. The guy chasing Hannah is, officially at least, an employee of the police in Santa Monica and he goes by the moniker 'Hawkeye.' We have to watch out for the possibility that he might try to get access to case information or even try to contact Kenny Brown and Jane Easton."

"Good point," Linda said. "Thanks. I'll put a note out to the police in Idaho Falls. With Jane out of the country that's not a priority, but I'll let the Atlanta police know it may be an issue in the future.

"Also," Linda said, "Jasmine is on her way back from Istanbul. She has done a lot of scouting there and with the help of Kram we have some very valuable material we will need soon. That includes the note about a big order we talked about. Oh, and finally," Linda added with emphasis, "tell Kram he cannot go down with a flu, or worse, until this case is closed. We need him around the clock."

"Will do," Eddie said.

"So, with all this in place, is *Peregrine* is ready for the next move?"

"Yes, Ma'am, we have everything. We're all ready for action."

CHAPTER THIRTY-TWO

THE BUSINESS SLOWED DOWN AS summer knocked on fall's door.

Matthew had not heard from Nicolas after the tense discussions in the past weeks and wondered if Nicolas might have taken the business to other parties. Matthew called Ron Patterson in California to see what he knew about the market.

Patterson called a few days later. He had recently met Nicolas at the marina in Santa Monica and chatted with him about business in general and about Gooding Bioenergy in particular.

"According to Nicolas, there seems to be caution and nervousness in the business with some of the operators. He even mentioned us by name," Patterson said. "He wasn't sure why that is, but he asked me to tell you that his grapevines in Europe have heard that we have good news coming in a day or two. A big order might be coming in from Turkey that we should prepare ourselves for. Nicolas will send more information soon."

"Awesome. Thanks Patterson, keep eyes and ears open on what happens in the market. We can still supply large quantities."

"Very good, Matthew."

A few days later, Nicolas called Matthew.

"Matt, how are things going in your end?" Nicolas said in an upbeat manner. "Haven't talked to you in weeks." They chatted about little things until Nicolas said, "Listen, we have a large order for B99 coming from Turkey. Not from the company we shipped stuff to some weeks ago, but, you know, the guy in Kocaeli near Istanbul that we did some business with in the past?"

"The guy with the cash problem that Ziraat Bankasi helped solve?"

"That's him! Always nice to have repeat customers. This time the deal is considerably larger." He wants to meet in Houston as soon as

119

possible.

"Great," Matthew said. "So, we finally get a chance to meet him face-to-face after all this time. I like that."

"Agree. What's your schedule like? I think we should fly out to Houston. Bring Hannah, by the way. She needs a vacation," Nicolas added.

"Nah, you know Hannah. She doesn't care much about business. She's a *cultural person*," Matthew said with poorly hidden, British-affected disrespect.

"Maybe if we *sail* to Houston she might like . . .?"

"I'll ask, but my guess is it's negative."

That evening, Matthew told Hannah he had to go to Houston and maybe other places for about a week to put a deal together. "I thought it might be a good idea if you come along," He added.

"Oh, Matt, you know how I feel about that. You guys will be in meetings all day long, go out to places at night that I don't really care for. Besides, I was actually thinking about attending the annual book fair in San Francisco, the biggest event in the Southwest. That starts next week."

"Yeah I know you like that stuff. But it would . . . Hey, you know what? We should go on a vacation together afterwards, or have a family gathering at a remote place. Do some of the things we used to do in earlier Toponis days."

"That sounds a lot more appealing to me. Plan your thing and I'll plan on going to San Francisco while you're gone."

"All right. That sounds good."

#

A letter from the *Kocaeli Yakıt Cmpany* arrived on Nicolas's fax machine, signed by Konst. Demirci, Başkan:

> *Dear Mr. d'Aubert,*
> *Kocaeli Yakıt Cmpany would like to buy 2.5 million gal*
> *B99 from Sirius and your Gooding partner.*
> *We have secured financial guarantees from Ziraat Bankasi*
> *in Ankara, a copy of which will be sent later today.*
> *If you can supply this quantity over the next 3 quarters,*
> *I would like to meet and discuss price and exact delivery*
> *schedule.*
> *We take the liberty to suggest a meeting in Houston next*

week if that is convenient for you.
Sincerely yours,
Konst. Demirci, Başkan.
Kocaeli Yakıt Cmpany - Kocaeli/Türk

Nicolas walked around in his office with his hands on his back. 'Like Prince Charles,' he reminded himself. He liked the comparison and it made him smile and feel good. 'We're getting to be the major player in USA, heck, probably anywhere in the world outside the Arab countries.'

Thirty minutes later, a separate email confirmed that funds would be available from Ziraat Bankasi. It was signed by the bank president, Mr. Bardakçı.

Nicolas went back to his computer and pulled up a translation website to see what Yakit, Cmpany, and Başkan was in English. He read:

- Yakit was Fuel
- Cmpany was Company
- Başkan was President

'So, Cmpany wasn't a typo as I thought. Interesting language.' But the content was in perfect English business language. And most importantly, Nicolas liked the content and contemplated how the deal could be constructed. He scanned the two faxes and attached them to an email to Matthew with a request to respond when he had had a chance to read them. A few minutes later Matthew wrote:

Awesome. Let's meet in Santa Monica before Huston.
It's a doable deal, but we need to do some planning.
Pls. suggest dates.

Nicolas's answer was prompt,
How about Monday?

A few hours later, Matthew emailed the flight schedule for coming to Santa Monica regional airport.

CHAPTER THIRTY-THREE

BRUCE 'HAWKEYE' WARNER CAME OUT of his motel to start his daily surveillance of Hannah. It was a search rather than a surveillance, he admitted to himself since there had been no signs of her for three days. He was not in the best of moods. The weather was windy and misty. 'It's pretty here but who in their right mind would want to live in a place like this when you can be in Santa Monica,' he thought as he half-walked, half-ran across the parking lot.

He stopped in his tracks.

'What the Hell?' He looked around. His rental car wasn't there. Bruce wondered if he absent-mindedly had parked on the other side of the building last night. 'It was dark, but not that dark. I had a couple of drinks, but that was all.' He walked around the motel. 'Dang.' It wasn't there either. He went into the lobby.

"Has there been any changes or work going on last night on the front parking lot?" he asked a young, heavily made-up Latino lady, who looked annoyed that no one had yet discovered her as the next big movie star.

"Not to my knowledge. Did you . . .?"

"My car is not where I parked it last night."

"Well, I guess someone must have . . ."

'*Of course* someone must have moved it,' Bruce almost said. 'The questions are who, why, and even how? AVIS, perhaps? Nah, why would they do that?' As if it would help his memory, Bruce spun around and walked back out to the parking lot. He looked around again, willing the car to appear. That's when he saw a small piece of paper on the ground with a small rock on it. *Bruce's P-lot. Reserved. Don't occupy.*

"Jesus Christ!" Bruce hissed. He realized in a flash that somebody knew he was in town, that the AVIS car was *his* rental, and knew where he stayed. That meant only one thing: *He* was being surveilled. 'But by whom?' he thought. 'The people Nicolas wants me to surveil? A cat-and-mouse game? But how would *they* know I'm in town. Actually, how would *anyone* know?'

He went back into the lobby.

"May I have a look at your surveillance camera with the recording from last night" he asked the aspiring movie star. Her badge read '*Monica*' in cursive.

"Um, I'm not sure. We're not allow to do that. That's for internal use only. I'll have to ask the manager for . . ."

Bruce pulled out his Santa Monica police badge. "I hope this helps," he said with a cold smile.

"I, eh, yeah, I guess so. Um . . . please follow me." She opened the side door in the reception desk and showed Bruce into a small room behind the reception. "What time interval are you interested in?"

"I came here around ten o'clock last night, so anywhere from that time and until this morning, say eight a.m.."

Monica rewound the video recorder to 9:45 p.m.. "Should we run it in double speed, or triple, perhaps?"

"Do triple first. If I see something I need to take a closer look at, we can re-run that segment." He sat down and Monica put the player in to fast replay. He expected it to be boring, and it was. A few cars arrived, owners got out, locked them, and disappeared into the lobby. He and his AVIS rental was one of them. Around eleven o'clock, one car left but nothing else happened.

Half an hour into the viewing, Monica asked if he wanted a cup of coffee. 'It could be a long night,' he thought, so he gratefully accepted. Five minutes later, he was served a cup of black coffee. "You're a sweetie. Thanks so much." He took a first sip and almost spilled the coffee while coughing.

"What the Hell is that?"

Monica turned around in the doorway. "Is it that bad?" she asked, clearly unhappy.

"No, no, not at all. But look! Go five minutes back and play it at normal speed." She did and sat down next to Bruce.

They leaned forward and stared open-mouthed when the AVIS car started, pulled out of the lot, and drove away . . . without a driver in it. The video timer read 11:46 p.m.

"What the Hell *is* that?" Bruce said again. Monica stared at him but didn't say anything. She couldn't see for sure if the car was empty.

"The video shows me getting out of the car around ten, and no one got into it afterwards. No one! How is that even possible?" he said, mostly to himself. He sat for another minute. "Thank you, Monica." He got up, gave her a kiss, and hurried out of the room. She stood with a smile on her face as if indeed she *had* just signed a movie deal. This was indeed the most exciting thing that had happened in and around Gooding in a long time, she thought.

Bruce went back to his room.

'Someone has the technology to hack the cars ignition, its computer steering, and then operate the pedals. I thought all that was sci-fi or at least only experimental technologies. I'm trying to find a domesticated, uneducated, allegedly unhappy, female member of the Toponis Order. No one knows I'm here. Still some invisible guy—or gal, of course—is on my back. 'Dang.'

Bruce hated the idea of reporting back to Nicolas on a situation like this. He would not be happy.

He was wrong.

Nicolas didn't go ballistic. He realized that not only was he as clueless as Bruce was, it struck him that this could be a sign that someone within his *own* organization was leaking information—maybe even among his own bodyguards, two of them being in jail already. Clearly, Bruce was now some sort of a target—and he didn't want go down the rabbit hole of guessing who was targeting him.

Most of all, the one remark Bruce was most surprised about was that Nicolas's was grateful for the fact that Bruce had had this experience and not himself.

"Hawkeye, you handled it a lot better than I would've," he said. "Move and get another car but keep doing what you're doing. We have no idea what kind of activity was behind this, but it teaches us that we must be extremely careful with everything we say and do. But you may have to use a heavy hand the first time you get an opportunity to do so."

CHAPTER THIRTY-FOUR

ALTHOUGH BRUCE'S SPIRIT WAS LIFTED a bit, the idea that Nicolas's was 'being extremely careful' bothered him. Often, it meant that *everyone* on the team was now a suspect, including himself.

Bruce got another car and drove to another motel and checked in. He was farther away from the Order but that didn't matter so much. Despite the weather, he loved the wooded area and didn't mind driving around. But what waited for him the next morning dampened his spirit.

When Bruce got into his car and was about to start the engine, he noticed a folded note under the passenger side's window wiper. He got out, grabbed the note and opened it.

It read,

> *Hi Hawkeye,*
> *Sorry we missed one another last night.*
> *Hope to meet you soon.*
> *Hannah*

Bruce was as furious as he was stunned. Someone was having him traced, successfully. Who manages to do that? He seriously doubted it was Hannah. From what he had been told, she was not an assertive, sophisticated person. Besides, her car never moved out of the garage, which he had under camera observation all the time. No, it had to be someone else with more than ordinary resources—manpower included —resources that included high-tech tools that could track his car and his whereabouts at all times, *and* who knew he was looking for Hannah. *That* was the worst part. *And* someone knew he's moniker was Hawkeye. That was known among only a few colleagues and friends back home. If this is the result of a leak,' Bruce thought, 'it goes back to Santa Monica.' It struck him that it might be Nicolas who was testing him. The mere thought of that possibility made him extremely uncomfortable—even when he tried to convince himself that it made no sense at all.

As Bruce kept wrestling with this problem, he concluded it could not be one individual. It had to be the local police or a local private detective working with the police. He had to add this trickster to his search. First priority was therefore to identify him . . . or her, maybe? Better yet, to pull this person within his own reach.

Since there really wasn't anything to report on the matter he was in Idaho for and he didn't want to include Nicolas in his thinking too early, he decided to send a very brief note back to Nicolas:

>*No signs of Hannah.*
>*This area is as deserted as Los Alamos after the blast.*
>*Bruce*

#

Two hundred miles away, Eddie smiled and texted Patrick and Linda.

#

All of the sudden, Bruce realized he had not watched very much of the video tape from the other night. He had, in other words, missed *who* had placed the note on the ground *after* the car had been moved. Bruce rushed back to the motel where the movie star was back behind the reception desk.

"Can I see the rest of the tape from the other night?" Bruce asked without any pleasantries.

"I'm sorry. The system self-erases and restarts the tape every morning around nine o'clock. We dont have a need for them for more than twenty-four hours."

Bruce stood for a moment. 'Dang! How could I be so stupid. C'mon, that's a beginner's mistake.' Then he went back to AVIS and put a third car on his contract. He had decided to visit Kenny Brown who was waiting for his trial to begin. Bruce would use his police badge to legitimize his visit. He looked up the central police station in Boise and called the front desk. A female officer answered. Bruce explained who he was and the purpose of his visit.

"I'll take care of that for you, Mr. Warner, if you can hold for a moment?" the officer said.

"I sure can, thank you."

"You're welcome. I'll be back in a sec."

'Long secs here in Idaho,' Bruce thought after three-four minutes had passed. He tapped his fingers on the armrest of his chair while listening to a maddening, looped jingle that was supposed to make him relaxed. When the officer came back, she said, "Mr. Warner? We have instructions not to allow any visitors to see Mr. Brown, but if you . . ."

"Ma'am, I'm with the LA police force. If you wish, I'll be happy to read the badge ID to you so you can check me out. I'm here for only for one day to convey some information to Kenny from his attorney."

"Hold on a moment. I need to make a phone call to get that clearance. Can I all you back in five-ten minutes?" Bruce OK'ed that.

When she called back, she said, "Sir, if you agree to having a supervising officer present when you visit with Kenny Brown, then we can do it for thirty minutes this afternoon at three o'clock or three-thirty. Will that be OK?"

"Perfect. I won't even need that much time. Thank you ma'am, I'll be there at three o'clock."

Bruce enjoyed the drive to Boise. The weather was finally pleasant and the wooded area was a nice chance from the LA scenery. He pushed the sunroof back and relaxed on the way. When he arrived, Bruce was greeted friendly, almost as if someone had hoped he would show up for a visit of this nature. That struck him as odd. He wasn't exactly a chief of police visiting from another city, but he pushed the thought out of his mind the minute he sat down with Kenny.

Kenny started by insisting the police had the wrong guy in the case against him and that he would be released soon.

"Did you discuss that with Nicolas?" Bruce asked.

"Oh, yes, he has the details. But . . ."

'What?' Bruce was stunned. 'Didn't Nicolas tell me he had no idea about why Kenny was in jail? Dang! What's that about?'

Kenny sensed there was an issue that he probably didn't want to be part of, and he decided to change the subject.

"Did you hear, by the way, that Jane is being transferred from Athens to Atlanta?" Kenny asked.

"No! Well, that's good news. At least she's in an American jail," Bruce said. "So, you have been in contact with her? How can you do that from here?"

"Strangely, we are both allowed to keep our phones. Other inmates here have to use the phones on the premises. Like I am, she's totally at loss with regard to her case, but she has warned us that someone must have a highly sophisticated technology and methodology to track people down."

"Tell me about it," Bruce said and told Kenny about his experiences the past 3-4 days. "Say, do you know anything about Hannah Smith?"

"I know the name and know she's the wife of the guy who runs the Gooding biofuel company, but other than that, I know nothing about her."

"Have you been in contact witht anyone from the Toponis Order?"

"No. Why do you ask?"

"Well . . ." Bruce thought about what Nicolas had said about Kenny's assignment. "I dunno. Didn't you try to chase Hannah down?"

Kenny looked like a questionmark. Bruce immediately pulled the antenna in and said instead, "I have a feeling Hannah or someone else is searching for me."

"Well, give her a call, then."

"I'm not sure that's a good idea?"

"Why not?" Kenny asked.

"Time," the officer in the back of the room said," and Bruce got up. "Let's stay in touch," he said. Kenny nodded, and Bruce walked out with more questions than he had before he got there.

#

Two hundred miles away, Eddie smiled and texted a thank you note to Patrick for being prescent and arranging a recording of Bruce's meeting with Kenny Brown.

#

That night, Hawkeye drove out to yet another motel in yet another car.

Yet, the next morning, when he looked out of the window, he saw a note under his window wiper. He got dressed, went downstairs, and opened the note:

Why do you keep changing cars?
And motels?
Hannah

Bruce clenched his teeth. This was beyond aggravating. That night, after another day of unsuccessfully searching for Hannah, he got into a new airbnb and sat in the window watching his latest rental car for eight frustrating hours. In the morning, groggy and stiff in his entire body he walked to the car. He smiled when there was no note under the window wiper.

But at 8:00 a.m., his phone vibrated with a message:

> *Good morning, Hawkeye*
> *Did you sleep well in that new airbnb?*
> *By the way, never mess with a person whose name*
> *can be spelled forward and backwards.*
> *Hannah*

CHAPTER THIRTY-FIVE

MEANWHILE, NICOLAS AND MATTHEW STARTED the planning of their biggest deal so far. After Matthew arrived in Santa Monica, they drove to Nicolas's estate home on Stone Canyon Road. It was the first time Matthew had visited Nicolas's home. 'Strange,' he thought, 'after all this time.'

Nicolas left the Lamborghini running in the driveway as he got out. Matthew, taller than Nicolas, struggled a bit getting out of the low-riding car. 'I guess his staff parks his cars,' Nicolas thought as they walked to the front door, which opened automatically. At that moment the garage door also opened and a young man came out, got into the Lamborghini, and parked it in the garage.

Nicolas didn't offer Matthew a tour of the house. Instead they went straight into his office and closed the door. While Nicolas went to the bathroom, Matthew looked around. It was an old, classic style office. A large mahogany desk and a maroon high-back leather chair dominated the room. Large, Persian area rugs were spread out on the bamboo floor, the couch and coffee table were of modern design, and behind the desk, a few colorful, non-figurative pieces of art—'originals without a doubt,' Matthew thought—stood out from the otherwise conservative style of the room. A large computer screen and a glass vase with fresh flowers was all that was on the desk.

'A weird mix of styles, Matthew thought. From the little he had learned from Hannah about decorating, Nicolas's focus was clearly on the value of individual pieces rather than on a uniform style.

"So, this is exciting," Nicolas started as soon as he sat down. "You saw the fax from Konstantin Demirci and the funding fax from the Ziraat bank. Konstantin has promised to bring the originals when we meet in Houston.

"Now, my question is: Can we handle a quantity as large as two-and-a-half million gallons?"

"Well," Matthew said, reflecting on how he could best answer it. He had thought about this since he first learned about it. "It's over three quarters, so it's definitely doable. We can start with the first several hundred thousand gallons and decide how we deal with the rest. The beauty is that we have a contract for multiple shipments but Konstantin doesn't specify how many. That gives us a lot of 'flexibility,'" Matthew fingered the quotation marks in the air, "if you know what I mean?"

"I'm glad to hear you haven't lost the touch, my friend. Yes, flexibility is what we look for. Should we do the Indian deal structure?"

That question took Matthew by surprise. Nicolas usually didn't ask for suggestions about how to do a deal. He always told how he wanted them done. 'Is he pulling me into a feel-good situation in an attempt to let my guards down on issues somehow related to the leak issue?' Matthew had not forgotten Hannah's comments about watching out for Nicolas and he didn't like the idea. 'But at least I'm not asked to strip down again.'

"I think that's a good idea," Matthew said with confidence. "We know how to do it, know how to structure it, and know what all the production documents, shipping documents, EPA credit applications, and banking papers should look like. Yes, let's copy that deal."

They spent the afternoon discussing the details of how they would address the supply of the B99 to Kocaeli. Timing would be the focus of the deal, and they agreed to send a fax to Konstantin about the meeting.

"Let's agree to meet in Houston, and since it's not until Monday we can have some time to go sightseeing." Nicolas certainly was upbeat. "On another matter. How about texting Hannah and tell her we will sail to San Fransisco and spend a couple of days on the Bay before we fly out?"

"Sure, but she'll be in a literary event of some kind. Big I believe."

"Ah, yes, I remember you mentioned that."

"Yes, and it starts sometime next week, so she may not even have left Gooding yet. Anyway, it runs all next week. I'd say, let's get this deal rolling according to what we have discussed here. We can celebrate it afterwards."

That agreed, Nicolas sent a text message to Konstantin. "I know it's midnight over there right now, but then his answer with flight information will get back to us tomorrow morning.

"Let's fly to Houston and spend a couple of days there before we meet Konstantin."

#

While Bruce was looking for Hannah in and around Gooding, Hannah had joined Katie in the airbnb that the FBI office in Salt Lake City had rented for Patrick. The airbnb was for three people and Hannah immediately got the impression that Patrick was there to be with Katie and not as much for safety. She smiled briefly and thought Katie was on the way to the happiness she had been robbed of not too long ago. She was happy for her but couldn't hide a trace of envy. Katie was free and happy.

She was neither.

The arrangement gave the three of them an opportunity to share up-to-date information on the investigation.

"The most important development is that we have been more than successful in applying Kram's Pegasus hacking tool," Patrick said to Hannah and Katie. "Kram has been messing with Bruce, who after a week's work has no leads in tracking you down, Hannah. Equally important, Kram has harassed Bruce with messages from you. It must drive him absolutely bonkers to realize *you* are chasing *him* while it should be the other way around. So, we expect . . ."

"Wait a minute," Hannah said, mouth open, moving her long hair away from her face. She combed her eyebrows with her fingers as she often did when she was under stress. Her face expressed concern rather than surprise. "I haven't sent *any* messages to this Bruce-guy. I know who he is and a little bit about what he does, but that's it. So, what d'you mean by . . ."

"*I* know you haven't sent anything, but Bruce doesn't know the messages are *not* from you. Most of them have, of course, been delivered by several of our officers at weird times of the day—or the night rather."

Hannah looked at Katie who shook her head. She sat back. "This is beyond me." She sounded defeated. Patrick patted her arm.

"Don't worry, Hannah, it's beyond me, too. Seriously! It's Eddie's friend, the Kram-guy and his secret network of super-techies, who knows how to do this hacking stuff. I don't know Kram personally and

I tend to believe we're better off not knowing how he does it. But I think we can have full confidence in him. Anyway, the point here is that Bruce gets messages that *appears* to be from you, Hannah, and that scares him because no one's supposed to know he's in Idaho."

"OK. That all sounds fine and dandy, but . . ." Hannah reflected on her situation for a moment and added, "I've been here for almost a week now; I like it here, I like to be with Katie, and I enjoy being with you, too, but still, despite all that, it feels sort of . . . like a prison. How long am I going to stay in hiding?"

She watched Katie's face. Katie didn't say anything and it confirmed in Hannah's mind that Katie actually was more than just comfortable with being under Patrick's protection.

After a moment, though, Katie seconded Hanna's worries. "Yes, it's weird not to be able to go out when and where you want to."

"As to how long?" Patrick said. "I don't have an exact answer. The FBI office in Salt Lake City is working on a plan that will resolve this situation very shortly," Patrick said hesitantly.

Katie picked up on that immediately. "What does that actually mean?"

"I would like to tell you but . . . I'm not in a position to do that."

CHAPTER THIRTY-SIX

NICOLAS AND MATTHEW SPENT A very pleasant weekend in Houston. The atmosphere was relaxed and they did not spend any time discussing business until Sunday night, when a text popped up on Nicolas's phone:

> Dear Mr. d'Aubert,
> May I suggest a meeting at Hyatt Place on Main Street
> on Tuesday at Noon. I'll be in the lobby wearing a
> maroon sports coat, reading the Houston Chronicle.
> I'll stay overnight. Gives us enough time to discuss
> business.
> Sincerely yours,
> K. Demirci

'So very formal—as always,' Nicolas thought and sent a confirmation mail right away.

#

Six hundred miles away, Eddie smiled and texted Patrick and Linda.

#

"OK, I thought it would be Monday morning, but good, we have another day to spend. Let's see what kind of sports events are on the program. Have you ever been to a Houston Astro's game?"

"Never. I'm not into baseball. But there's a first time for everything. So, let do that if there's a home game on."

There was, and they had a good evening, including dinner and visiting night clubs with live music into the early morning.

"Why don't you have a yacht here?" Matthew asked when they walked back to the hotel. "You are here so often."

"I thought about it but it's hard to get the people you need and trust to take care of them. So, I only have the one in Santa Monica and one on Cyprus. That's enough. On the other hand, if we have more meetings here, maybe I *should* get a third one."

#

Tuesday morning, Nicolas and Matthew drove to Main Street, parked in the underground garage of Hyatt Place, and took the elevator up to the main lobby.

Konstantin Demirci was already there, easy to spot in his maroon sports coat and the newspaper under his left arm, watching the fish in the huge, cylindrical aquarium in the center. His briefcase was at his feet.

Demirci looked up when he heard the approaching footsteps on the marble-tiled floor and put out his hand to greet Nicolas and Matthew.

"Great to meet you both," Demirci said. "Glad we could arrange this,"

"Likewise," Nicolas and Matthew said in unison.

Demirci was 5'8". He looked fit like a runner. His hair, beard and full, curved eyebrows were thick and almost black. He had a dark complexion. He was the stereotype of a Slavian or East-european person, they both thought.

"Shall we?" Demirci pointed in the direction of the lunch area. "I have reserved a meeting room for the afternoon, so let's get a bite to eat first."

"Very well," Nicolas said as he and Matthew followed Demirci.

After ordering their lunch, the conversation that followed was entirely about backgrounds, educations, a bit about careers, and hobbies. Fishing was Demirci's main leisure time activity.

"I love everything with the ocean, rivers, lakes. I'm fortunate to be close to all of that," Demirci said, something Nicolas definitely could relate to.

Demirci was lively and eloquent, clearly well traveled, and, with both a high school education in Massachusetts, a degree from MIT, and a couple of years with a small oil company in New England, his English was polished and almost free from an accent. The three men clicked well from the get go, and the atmosphere was the very best as they got up and went to the meeting room on the Executive Floor.

"Here's my business card," Demirci said and passed two cards across the table to Nicolas and Matthew. Nicolas reciprocated while Matthew apologized for having run out of his cards. Nicolas studied the company logo on the business card. He liked the logo that he remembered from the letterhead.

"So, is there any meaning to the word Demirci? I know a lot of Turkish surnames refer to trades or handcrafts," Nicolas asked.

"Indeed. Demirci means blacksmith, and comes from the craft of my father and his forefathers. Actually, my father wanted me to be a blacksmith, too, but I wanted to study abroad."

"Interesting. I don't think d'Aubert means anything, but Matthew's last name, which is Smith, also means . . . smith." Demirci smiled.

Demirci pulled out from his briefcase the letter that was faxed to Nicolas as well as the bank support letter from Ziraat Bankasi. "Here are the originals, just so we have all the formalities in order."

The three men discussed quantities, time tables, deadline for the applications needed to process the international trade.

"Tell me about your production," Demirci said. "How did you get into that business. If I'm not mistaken, Idaho is not exactly know as a location for large productions—unless it's potatos, I guess." His smiled showed he was proud of his knowledge about the state. They all laughed.

"Yes and no," Matthew said. "Industry-wise, no, but we are close to a lot of the crops we need for the biofuel, so in that sense it's a very good place." Matthew proudly showed photos of the facility and explained the production capacity and the flexibility they had, which would accommodate Demirci's need for smaller and more frequent deliveries.

Everything clearly impressed Demirci, who explained that the Turkish bank preferred many smaller deals over one or two large ones because of the more limited risk involved in each shipment.

"Oh, thanks for reminding me . . . I also brought a few photos from our facility which, of course, is mostly tanks, a fleet of trucks, etc.. All relatively small, nothing eh, what do you call it? Fancy, I think? But all necessary." Matthew nodded.

The rest of the day was spent on discussing delivery schedule. Demirci pretty much agreed with what Matthew suggested, who added that "all this is depending on the 'approval' by the production manager, who knows the production plans for the next three monts better than I do. But let's stick to this for now."

The three men were happy with the meeting and enjoyed the dinner afterwards, too. As they broke up, they decided to meet for breakfast the next morning to catch up on last minute details before Demirci had an early morning flight out of Houston.

As they parted the next day, Nicolas and Matthew agreed they would get to work on all the documents and get the first shipment underway as soon as possible.

They went to the airport, where Nicolas flew back home on his own plane and Matthew boarded an Alaska Airlines flight to Idaho.

#

With a large, multi-delivery deal on the order books, Matthew decided to make the deal into a six-shipment deal, and he started drafting six installments to be implemented over the next nine months.

After the OK from the production manager, Matthew planned the first shipment to be based on an actual shipment, and the identification number for the credit from EPA and IRS would be declared according to existing rules.

For the following three shipments, Matthew would buy several hundred shipping containers of B99 from dealers in Colorado, Texas, and New Mexico, relabel it as used waste oil from the food business, ship it to the *east* coast of Panama. There, it would be unloaded onto trucks, hauled to the *west* coast of Panama, reloaded and sent to Gooding Biofuels, where the documents would show it was processed into the B99 it was in the first place. That would generate identification numbers and tax credits of more than $200,000 gallons per shipment without doing anything.

For the last two of the six shipments, Matthew prepared documents that showed that Gooding Energy would produce 200,000 gallons biodiesel for each of them although the actual amount that Demirci needed was much smaller. And then, Matthew would rotate the shipments in a circle from port to port in California, Texas and Louisiana. Gooding Bioenergy would claim credits on the same batch of fuel three times.

Matthew sat back after two long days in the office. It was a lot of papers but he had all the fabricated invoices, production records, and bills of lading for all the legitimate shipments generated in the process. 'A convincing package,' he thought, congratulating himself with a job well done. He sent an a email to Nicolas outlining the deal step by step and reminded him of the conversation they had had few years ago, where Nicolas had finished a similar planning by saying, 'Why go through all the trouble of actually *moving* tons of products thousands of miles, when you can just make the documents *showing* that you were doing it—and make money on the paperwork.'

When Nicolas had read the email, checked the procedure and the steps he and Matthew had to complete, he smiled, poured himself a whisky, and sent a mail back saying, 'Awesome job. You have not lost your touch. I'll confirm all of it to Konstantin Demirci.'

After sending a fax to Demirci, Nicolas decided to spend the evening on *Sirius* on Santa Monica Bay and maybe have dinner at Malibu Point.

CHAPTER THIRTY-SEVEN

AS SOON AS PATRICK PICKED up the information that Hawkeye was back in Santa Monica and nothing indicated he was being substituted by another bodyguard, he discussed the situation with Katie and Hannah. They had stayed in the airbnb with Patrick for ten days now, and with Matthew coming back from traveling, it was imperative that Hannah went back home.

Katie could not hide the fact that she looked forward to being alone with Patrick even though it meant she would not have the daily contact with Hannah in the future.

Patrick had anticipated questions from Hannah about how she could 'prove' she had been in San Francisco. He had already arranged with Eddie and Kram how to document her stay. Besides the receipt for her participation in the literary conference, Hannah had the airline reservation tickets, hotel bills, tabs from restaurants and bars, as well as entry tickets to a few entertainment places in and around San Francisco, all paid for with her credit card.

Patrick had also supplied Hannah with information of tourists spots she definitely would have visited, like the Presidio, the Golden Gate Bridge, the Alcatraz, and the charming steep and super-winding Lombard Street so she could talk intelligently about them. After she had looked up photos from these tourist destinations on the Internet, she almost felt like she had been there. 'What a weird scenario,' she thought, 'sitting in an airbnb in Idaho feeling like I've been there. How do these guys do what they do?' she wondered anew.

"I'd love to go back there one day," she said convincingly to Matthew when she had finished talking about her trip over dinner. Matthew could tell Hannah was excited, and he was happy to hear she had enjoyed herself on her very first time on the West Coast.

"Well, I'm sure that can be arranged," Matthew responded and then told Hannah bits and pieces about his trip to Houston and some of the work that was ahead of the company. "We'll be busy in the next many weeks," he said.

Hannah nodded, struggling with appearing interested.

#

And busy he was.

He had long conversations with Nicolas and long meetings with Isaiah, whose frown became deeper and deeper over the business of Gooding Bioenergy. He was stressed and had lost weight in the past six months, and his incessant readjusting of the Lennon-glasses on his long nose bridge had become a nervous tick.

Hannah observed it silently. She, too, was becoming increasingly nervous about what was going on. She understood a big deal was underway, and a couple of secret messages from 'Macki' via Katie's library books indicated that 'an important meeting was coming up soon.'

Whatever it was, she hoped it would be soon—and over with soon.

#

"Lots of things will happen very fast in the next few days and weeks, beginning right this moment," Linda said at the start of a meeting with everyone involved in Project *Peregrine*.

She was reading an email from Demirci at Kocaeli Yakıt Cmpany to Sirius/Nicolas:

> *The first shipment to our company has not arrived.*
> *Puts us in a very difficult situation.*
> *I insist on a meeting in Houston as soon as possible.*
> *Please confirm.*
> *K. Demirci*

Less than a minute after receiving the email, Nicolas sent this note back to Demirci. Linda read it:

> *KD: What are you talking about?*
> *We shipped the fuel according to the plan we made in Houston.*
> *We have confirmation from you that the shipment arrived.*
> *Pls. explain - N d'A*

"That prompted an immediate reaction," Linda said, "but not one Nicolas had expected.".

> *Not from my company!*
> *K. Demirci*

"I can imagine how furious and in utter disbelief Nicolas is." She put the three emails down. "I must say that the success so far in the *Peregrine* project is a result of the masterful work of everyone in our group. Eddie, please tell your mysterious buddy, Kram, that we would like to meet him. We could not have accomplished what we have accomplished without him." Eddie nodded.

"Now, while Nicolas is pulling his hair out, Demirci will send a note to Nicolas, telling him when he wants to meet. What day and time suit everyone?" Linda asked.

"Anytime," was the firm reply from around the table. This was the top priority among all their tasks.

"Can we be ready for a meeting in Houston this Friday morning at 10:00 a.m.?"

"Absolutely," was the response. Everyone made notes to that effect.

"OK, so I'll suggest that."

Everyone got up. Their was a lot each one had to do in the next two days.

An hour later, a fax ticked in on Nicolas's office machine:

> *Dear Mr. d'Aubert,*
> *May I suggest we meet on Friday at 10:00 a.m..*
> *Same hotel as last time.*
> *I'll be in the lobby.*
> *Sincerely yours,*
> *K. Demirci*

Minutes later, Linda had Nicolas's confirmation to Demirci.

CHAPTER THIRTY-EIGHT

WITH 3-1/2 HOUR FLYING TIME to Houston and an hour to get to the hotel at that time of the day, Nicolas—accompanied by Bruce Hawkeye and Stan, who'd much rather be on *Sirius 2* on Cyprus—left Santa Monica airport very early in the morning on his Cessna. Since Matthew had chosen to go there the night before, he picked Nicolas and company up at the airport in an uber car and drove straight to the garage under Hyatt Place.

When the four of them got up to the lobby area, Nicolas and Matthew immediately spotted Demirci, who wore the same maroon sports coat as last time and had the Houston Chronicle in front of him.

Demirci got up when he saw Nicolas, Matthew and two bodyguards approach.

"Shall we?" he said and pointed towards the elevator. Except for a few words about the flight from Santa Monica, there was no small talk on the way up to the business mezzanine floor or down the hallway to the meeting room. The tension was palpable.

Nicolas and Matthew sat down on one side of the conference table and put their documents in front of them. Bruce and Stan picked two of the four chairs lined up along the wall behind Nicolas and Matthew. Demirci sat down on the opposite side of the table.

"I have a couple of colleagues with me," Demirci said, "but let's get started and see where we are before we call them in."

Nicolas nodded his consent. His foul mood prevented him for engaging in any pleasantries, and he went directly to the outstanding point.

"So, you sent this email informing us that the first shipment under our contract had not arrived. And I sent a note back telling you that we have a confirmation letter from your company on my desk. And *then* you told me that *that* was not the case. What's going on here?"

"Neither one of these two faxes are to or from my company," Demirci responded tersely.

"Nonsense. They most certainly are. Look . . ." Nicolas pushed the two faxes across the table. "Isn't this your company?"

"It sure looks like they are. Name and logo are the same. But as you know yourself very well, a business card, letterheads, logos, and so on don't really tell who you are. So, no! Kocaeli Yakıt Cmpany never sent or received those emails."

Nicolas sat back in the chair with a murderous look. The barb about false business cards bothered him. What did he know? He put his speculations aside.

"So . . . who sent them?"

"*I* did." The words hung ominously in the air.

Nicolas's eye narrowed to mere slits as he leaned forward. "What the Hell . . . Are you playing with words here? 'My company' didn't sent the letter, but 'I did,'" Nicolas said in a mocking caricature of Demirci's tenor voice. Did someone else in your company communicate with us without your knowing it? Give me a break. As far as I'm concerned, your company and anyone in it are the same in regards to the deal we have. If I were an English teacher I could perhaps see the difference, but . . .

Nicolas had the feeling he was being trapped but didn't know how he could wiggle himself out of it. At the moment, he didn't have the presence of mind to ask what had happened to the shipment that actually *had* taken place. Instead, he grasped at the only thing that looked like an explanation.

"So, are you telling me that there's no Konstantin Demirci and no Kocaeli Yakıt Cmpany in Turkey?"

"Oh, no! Not at all," was the answer. "There absolutely *is* a Kocaeli Yakıt Cmpany with a Mr. Demirci as its CEO. You did some business with them some years ago. And Jasmine visited that company, by the way, right after she had lunch on *Sirius 2*." Nicolas didn't see Stan jerking up in his chair, looking totally bewildered.

"Jasmine? Who's . . .?" Nicolas asked.

"We'll get back to Jasmine in just a minute. So, yes, she visited with the *real* Konstantin Demirci, got information about his company, and took the photos of his facilities I showed you at the last meeting. But in the last couple of months, you never communicated with Konstantin Demirci. You dealt with *me*. And I don't own Kocaeli Yakıt—or any other company in Turkey for that matter."

"What kind of nonsense is that?" Nicolas asked exasperated. Matthew was ashen-gray and looked completely lost. He had a strong, nagging feeling that this Turkish guy, whomever he was, had the facts correct. But how? 'There's no doubt he's Mr. Demirci,' Matthew convinced himself. 'We communicated with him for weeks and we . . .' He decided to narrow the discussion down to that simple fact.

"So, when we met a few weeks ago," Matthew attempted, "in this very room, and . . ."

"You didn't meet with Konstantin Demirci from Kocaeli Yakıt . . ."

"This is beyond absurd. What kind of game is that?" Nicolas seconded Matthew.

"Same game as you're playing," Demirci said calmly.

"And what the Hell's that s'posed to mean?' Nicolas slammed his hand on the table. "Clarify that if you can."

"You're not whom you pretend to be."

"Meaning?"

"You're not Marquis Nicolas d'Aubert."

"Oh, no?" Nicolas jerked back in his chair, then leaned forward. "So, who in your fucking smartass opinion am I?"

"You are Nicolas Ionescu, born and raised in Escondido near San Diego by Romanian parents. A middle school dropout who worked long hours for ten years at various gas stations to eke out a living— very commendable, of course—all while dreaming of having French nobility roots. When you read about IRS and EPA giving out credits for biofuel the same way these agencies do for solar panels and windmills, you devised a credit scam, which you implemented with Matthew Smith, whom you needed in order to lend credibility to the notion that you had manufacturing capacity. Early on, in your rise, you moved from Escondido to Commerce on the southside of Los Angeles, changed your name and image to match your ambitions, and soon, long story short, you were a very wealthy man living in Santa Monica. That's it—in a nutshell."

Nicolas was seething as he heard those words and wrestled with them. But he didn't connect with them as he stared into the emptiness. His face was impossible to read.

"What a delightful story," Nicolas finally said with a facetious smile and without looking at Demirci when he spoke. "Why don't you go to Disney with that story. They love fantasies." He sat for another moment as if to plan a new strategy.

"So, since *you* are not Mr. Demirci from Turkey, who are you?" Nicolas shot back.

"I'm agent Eddie Galway at the FBI Criminal Justice Information Services in the Salt Lake City Field Office." Eddie showed him his FBI badge, "and I have my boss, Linda Barnes in the room next to this one together with a couple of our colleagues."

"What a bunch of bullshit," Nicolas said dismissively. "You want me to believe that?" His eyes became slits again. "So, instead of wasting our time with more crap, tell me why FBI all of the sudden is interested in tax money? I did't think . . ."

"Sure. There are two answer to that. One: We have been *asked* by IRS to assist in investigating fraudulent transactions worth more than 600 million dollars. Two: We are here to arrest you for the ordering of and paying for two murders and attempting a third."

There was a flash of horror in Nicolas's eyes before he started laughing hysterically. Eddie let him be for a moment. Matthew turned to Nicolas in utter disbelief. "What the Hell is he talking about? Murders?" he asked.

"I've no idea. By the way, I changed my mind. Go to Hitchcock's studios instead of Disney,"Nicolas said as he locked eyes with Eddie. "They may like your crime plot." He sat for another moment before he asked, "And who are those unfortunate, fictitious victims supposed to be."

"I'll have my colleagues answer that question," Eddie said and pressed the button on the conference intercom in the center of the table. The clear tone came through after just a few seconds.

"Linda, would the three of you join us in here, please."

A moment later, Patrick and Jasmine walked in and sat down next to Eddie. Linda got in last and sat down at the end of the table.

The moment froze.

CHAPTER THIRTY-NINE

FROM HIS POSITION BEHIND NICOLAS, Stan stared at Jasmine with his mouth open and total disbelief painted all over his face.

"You?"

"Yes, nice meeting you again, Stan. How's your knee?"

Nicolas spun around and faced Stan. "What? D'you two know each other."

"Not really," Stan said feebly.

"We've met only once," Jasmine hastened to add. "We had lunch on *Sirius 2* before I went to see Kocaeli Yakıt Cmpany outside Istanbul. That's all." Jasmine smiled and turned to Stan. "Thanks, by the way. I think I forgot to say that when I left." Stan looked at Jamine with a trace of 'I'll be darned'-admiration. When she held his stare, he looked down and scowled. 'This will not end well,' he thought.

Bruce Hawkeye Warner stared at Patrick and pointed a finger in his direction. "You? You were in Boise when . . .?"

"When you saw Kenny Brown," Patrick completed his question. "That's right. I was the supervising officer. Sorry it was for such a short time and that we didn't have a chance to chat."

Nicolas turned the other way around and stared at Hawkeye with his mouth open. "What the Hell is he talking about?"

Nicolas didn't wait for the answer as he had a feeling it was perhaps better not to know. The thought of an insider mole came rushing back to him. Instead of giving in to that thought, he tried to control his anger and compose himself. Assuming Linda was the boss, he turned to her.

"We have already wasted an hour on this fabricated nonsense. I've had enough and have no time for more fairy tales." Give me just one shred of evidence that I, meaning Matthew and I, have anything to do with all these fabrications—or I'm out of here." He gathered his papers in front of him making it look like he was ready to leave, but he leaned back in his chair and crossed his arms in front of his chest, convinced he could call Linda's bluff.

"Oh, sure. We'll be glad to," Linda said calmly. "Where do you want us to start?"

There was no response from Nicolas or Matthew.

"Very well," Linda said. "Let's talk about the two murder victims. Lets start with Brian Carlson and the car bombing." She looked and gestured towards Patrick.

 Patrick cleared his throat.

"Well, Brian Carlson was accidentally killed when his car was blown up by a plastic explosive planted underneath it. The perpetrator was one of *Sirius*'s fixers, a Mr. Kenny Brown. I say 'accidentally,' because Katie Carlson was the intended target. Brian happened to be in the wrong place at the wrong time." Patrick went through the details of the GPS location on Kenny Brown's phone.

When that, as Patrick expected, was dismissed by Nicolas as pure fabrications, Patrick replayed the recordings obtained by the IMSI system in Nicolas's office. Everyone heard Nicolas's voice ordering Kenny Brown to cause a bomb explosion of Katie and Brian's car just outside Idaho Falls at a time Katie would be expected to be in it.

"Questions?" Linda asked. "Oh, before I forget and for the sake of good order, I should mention that a copy of this recording has already been filed with a judge, just in case something should happen to Patrick's phone."

There was a long silence in which Nicolas sat stone-faced. Matthew was in total disbelief. His lips moved as he whispered Katie's name. It was as if he were on a different planet listening to people he didn't know filling the room with words he couldn't understand. It was entirely surreal. The atmosphere was heavy with tension.

"Very well," Linda said and continued. "Let's move on. The other murder victim was Dan Hancock in Atlanta. Eddie, will you talk about that?"

"Yes. In this case the perpetrator was a woman living southwest of Atlanta. Her name is Jane Easton, whom Jasmine framed in Nicosia's airport. We have the exact same data on her as we have on Kenny Brown. GPS data on her phone correspond with the exact location and exact time when the control of Dan Hancock's car was taken over by an external computer, which made the car fail to brake as it was heading into a sharp right curve—and cause a collision with a large tree. The police in Atlanta has confirmed our investigation results. Further, we have phone communication with Nicolas's office about how to make the sabotage of the car look like an accident. Should we replay that conversation here?"

Eddie looked at Nicolas, then at Matthew, and then back at Nicolas. "No? Very well. And as Mrs. Barnes just said, the judge has a copy of that recording, too, so we can play it in court."

There was another long silence. Nicolas didn't look at Matthew, who half-whispered, "So, it *was* you who did that? And you lied about it." Nicolas didn't react.

"OK," Linda, said again. "Let's go to the attempted murder case, then. Patrick, will you give us a summary."

"Sure," Patrick said. "Without going into a lot of details, unless we have to: The intention behind a week long manhunt in the region around the Toponis Order was the elimination of Hannah Smith." Patrick laid out each and every communication to Bruce Warner's phone, details of his car rentals, lodging, and his moving around in the Gooding area as he kept missing Hannah. "Mr. Hawkeye, sitting right there, can explain what I mean by that. And that was despite the fact Hannah left messages for him almost every morning. Let me correct that: That's what *Bruce* thought. The hunt was unsuccessful *not* because Bruce didn't do a good job or try hard enough *but* . . . because Hannah wasn't close. Nor was she in San Francisco, by the way, as Matthew believed."

Nicolas sat stone-faced.

Bruce's face was unreadable, too, as he wrestled with some pieces now falling into place. 'That answers the questions I had when I met Kenny in Boise. Nicolas lied to both Kenny and me.'

Stan looked from Jasmine to Eddie to Patrick and back to Jasmine. When she caught his eyes, he looked away.

Matthew was lost. He had seen the brochures, the hotel and restaurant receipts on the credit card statement. None of this made sense, but he didn't know how to challenge it because his mind was completely absorbed in the surreal situation that assaulted him. In a sudden surge of rage, Matthew turned to Nicolas. "You. Ordered. Hannah. To. Be. Murdered? . . . How *could* you?" he hissed. His eyes reflected unfathomable disbelief, the blood vessels in his temples pulsed, and the knuckles on his hands were white. Linda thought for a moment Matthew would get up and start pounding on Nicolas.

"Seriously?" Nicolas said. "Are you buying all this nonsense, Matt? C'mon, I thought you were smarter than that." There was no reaction to this from Matthew. He was emprisoned in the web of lies laid bare before him. He could see the pieces of a huge, complex puzzle fall into place. He literally withered away in that moment.

"Gentlemen?" Linda said as an invitation to Nicolas and Matthew and their bodyguards to say something. "Anything to add? Any comments or questions? We have all the time you need."

Linda had expertly used the pauses to increase the pressure on Nicolas's team: They were paralyzed from not knowing what might come next. There was nothing more to be said. The silence was eerie. Everyone was watching everyone else.

'Something's going to happen,' Patrick thought. He intensely watched the subtle motions of the stone-faced men on the other side of the table. All waiting.

He prepared himself.

CHAPTER FORTY

IN A MOTION OF EXPLOSIVE force, Nicolas, who had had both hands under the edge of the conference table, lifted his side of the table way up on it's edge and forcefully pushed it on top of Linda's team. Phones, intercom, laptops, water bottles, glasses, papers, and a dozen folders flew into the air and crashed behind and around them.

Nicolas jumped on the top of the upside-down table and with a huge leap landed on the floor, got up, and flung the door open. Matthew, Stan, and Bruce jumped to their feet. Bruce had his gun drawn. Matthew stood paralyzed and watched the unfolding chaos, wide-eyed and with his left hand covering his mouth.

Linda and Eddie both fell over backwards and were partly covered by their chairs and the table. Patrick and Jasmine were on the floor, too, but free to move. Patrick saw the black handgun that Bruce pointed in his direction. Assuming Stan had drawn a gun, too, he and Jasmine knew in a flash that to save their colleagues and themselves, they had to take on Stan and Bruce and let Nicolas escape.

Patrick immediately fired at Stan who was directly across from him, taking him down with a single shot to his abdomen while Jasmine rapid-fired two shots at Bruce who was directly across from her. Patrick and Jasmine waited a moment with their guns ready to fire again if the two bodyguards might react, but Bruce seemed lifeless and Stan had crumbled into a fetal position in a pool of blood, moaning and holding his arms across his stomach, making no signs of getting up.

Meanwhile, Nicolas disappeared through the door and the sound of running feet quickly got fainter.

Before even getting up and ignoring the blood, drenched clothes, and frazzled looks, Linda went into operation mode.

"Eddie and Patrick, give chase and make your plans on the run." They immediately disappeared out of the room and ran down the hallway towards the elevators.

Even before she got to her feet, Linda said, "Jasmine, you and I stay here. I'll call for ambulances and police. You double check on Bruce and Stan." She got up slowly, ignoring the pain in her body, found her phone on the floor, and made the 911-calls.

Jasmine moved chairs and debris aside. With a quick look at Matthew, she knew it was not hard to keep him in check. Jasmine wondered for a second if he was in cardiac arrest, but concluded that a state of shock had immobilized him. With her gun in hand she turned to Bruce who had collapsed under the table. Zero pulse confirmed he had died immediately. Then she turned to Stan.

Stan's breathing was labored and slow, but he was conscious. When Jasmine moved his arms from his belly to the sides, she noticed that a large, heavy metal buckle on his 'cowboy belt' was badly damaged by a penetrating bullet. 'It may have saved his life—for now, at least,' Jasmine thought. When she bent over him to check his pulse, he lifted his head off the floor and looked up and into her eyes, attempting a smile. Jasmine thought she heard him whisper "I'm sorry . . . for . . . for what . . ." but he grimmaced, closed his eyes, and lowered his head to the floor to save his energy.

#

Nicolas had caught the elevator going down from the mezzanine to the lobby just as the door shut. He assessed his situation. He knew instinctively that going up would make him a sitting duck and going down to the garage floor would force him into the arms of the police who would try to prevent him from stealing a car. In other words, he could not get to his Cessna in the airport ahead of the police.

That left him with one alternative only: He had to get out of the hotel building from the engine room in the basement or find a hiding spot where he could wait it out until it became dark outside—and then go.

The elevator stopped at 'Lobby.' No one entered and Nicolas pressed B and continued down to the basement.

He had taken off his sports coat and pulled a rainbow-colored bandana from the side pocket. He wrapped it around his forehead and completely covered his hair. With that and his dark-green polo shirt, he knew he looked like an ordinary guy on the street that people would pass by.

As the doors opened and he entered the basement, he threw his jacket in a large trash bin on the backside of the elevator shaft.

Eddie and Patrick stopped for a second when they reached the elevators. "He's too savvy to go up," Eddie speculated. "He knows he would be trapped. I bet he went to the garage floor to steel . . . No, I take that back. He has gone to the basement. Let's go." Instead of waiting for the elevators to come to the mezzanine floor, they ran down the stairs next to them.

"We need reinforcement to block all exits," Eddie said. "I'll get a floor plan from the reception desk and meet you in the basement." With powerful strides, he disappeared.

When Patrick got to the basement, he stood still for at least a couple of minutes, listening for the slightest sound that could give away a spot where Nicolas could be hiding. There was no rattling of metal, no footsteps to hear, no breathing, no flash lights moving, nothing. It was almost completely dark. Only the red EXIT signs added enough light to navigate after his eyes had accommodated the darkness. Patrick found a set of light switches on the wall of the elevator shaft, but they didn't turn on any light.

Eddie came back a few minutes later. "No floorplans. We must improvise." As Patrick went towards one end of the basement, Eddie went to the other. More than 15 min went by before Eddie sent a vibrating buzz to Patrick's phone to signal they should meet. Under their breaths, they talked about their options.

All of a sudden, they heard footsteps. They stepped to the side and saw a hotel service man in blue overalls approaching, toolbox in hand and smudge on his cheeks. "Howdie," the man said when he saw Eddie and Patrick.

"Excuse me," Eddie said. "Have you by any chance seen another service man down here. We can't find anything in this darkness. We need to . . . "

"Sure," the service man said in a rather feminine voice. "We had to cut the power but I'm putting it on again if you can wait a minute. So, he's still over there where the compressors are . . ." He pointed with a dirty hand into the dark end of the basement. "He's in the room where it says 'Staff Only' on the door—right next to the service elevators and stairs. I'd call him if I had my phone with me."

"Don't think about it. We'll find him," Eddie said. They thanked the man and headed in the direction of the compressors. They walked slowly as the didn't want to give their own positions away by using the lights of their smart phones to guide them.

"Wait! Stop!" Patrick stood for a second.

"What?"

"Jesus! That was Nicolas."

"Nicolas? What? Are you . . . How d'you know that? He looked nothing like . . ." Eddie said with a hint of skepticism. They didn't have time to follow dead end leads. "We need to get . . ."

"His aftershave! It's *Brut*. I noticed it right away when we walked into the conference room. A very distinct, very sweet fragrance. Popular twenty years ago. My brother-in-law uses it all the time, and I hate it. That guy smelled like my brother-in-law. And I doubt very much a service man uses such an expensive after shave—on the job no less.

"Let's go."

Patrick led them back fromt where they had met the service man, who already had disappeared from the basement.

#

Nicolas took off the blue overalls and wiped his face with one of the pants. In his polo shirt, rainbow bandana, sunglasses pushed up on the forehead, and hands in his pockets, he entered the lobby and stopped right outside the door. 'Thank goodness. I bet it's only a matter of minutes before the police arrive,' he thought and casually exited the Hyatt Place and disappeared around the corner of Main Street.

When he and Eddie met Linda in the lobby, Eddie asked her hopefully, "Did you see him?".

"Here?" Linda shook her head.

"Dang! We lost him," Patrick said and almost stamped his foot.

CHAPTER FORTY-ONE

"DON'T WORRY, WE'LL GET HIM," Linda said. "Sooner or later," she added. "You made him confirm he arrived on his own Cessna this morning, and must have gotten to the hotel in a taxi or uber, so we know he doesn't have a car—unless he steals one. Smart thinking, Patrick. He can't fly out because he knows we'll nab him if he tries. He'll be on foot for a while.

"I texted my secretary already to have the local police initiate a Blue Alert, so all toll roads will be monitored—although we don't know yet if he stole a car. Also, all hotels and inns will be monitored for registrations, and so on. One of the few photos we have of Nicolas will be circulated throughout Texas immediately and throughout the country early tonight. That should close access to airports for the next couple of days. We know Nicolas is savvy so he may still slip through the cracks, but that's the best we can do.

"If you, Eddie, contact Kram, we can monitor all credit card movements, bank charges, et cetera. Have him monitor Zelle and PayPal as well. Because he lost his phone in the chaos upstairs, he's away from the surveillance system he has been under for a while, but there's nothing we can do about that for the moment.

"Let's go back up to the conference room to Jasmine. She's holding up Matthew and the bodyguards until the police arrives. They should be here any moment."

When the police, led by Captain Hales, showed up, Linda reported all the details of the events. Captain Hales took charge from there. "We'll finish up all the routine work starting now," he started. "Our people will make sure Matthew is transferred into our custody right away and Bruce to the morgue. We will take Stan to St. Joseph Medical Center and hope he survives. If so, we'll talk with him tomorrow or in the next few days. Finally, we will notify Interpol tonight about Nicolas Ionesco, alias d'Aubert, being wanted for double murder.

"Anything else of immediate importance?" Captain Hales asked.

"Yes, Linda said. "We need to close all loopholes in this area where Nicolas could access the coastline, that's all the way from Galveston down to Brownesville. He's a yachtsman, so he may try to get away on a vessel, possibly by stealing one. Ideally, we need to let all marinas in that area know that Nicolas is not allow to rent boats. We need a photo distributed to them ASAP.

"Together with the team in Salt Lake City," Linda finished, "I will coordinate the rest of the national search and keep the contact with Interpol."

With nothing else raised, they all got up. Hales left and Linda asked everyone to stay at Hyatt Place until the next day, maybe longer. "We should meet for breakfast tomorrow," she said, "so we can coordinate any information we may have obtained between now and then."

That agreed, Linda booked rooms for the night for each one of them. After forming a speed calling group for texting, they separated. On the way to their rooms, Patrick asked Linda if he should contact Hannah right away, but Linda wanted to wait until after breakfast the next day.

#

Tasks were assigned to everyone during the breakfast.

Linda and Eddie, with the support of Kram, would coordinate with Captain Hales how to track Nicolas down. It was agreed that Jasmine would go to the hospital to check in on Stan—"since you guys already know one another," Linda said with a crooked smile.

Patrick prepared himself to go back to Idaho Falls but before he checked out, he called Hannah.

#

Hannah was working with Isaiah in the office when the phone rang.

Hannah, I have some, eh, serious news. Patrick hesitated so long that Hannah said, "Yeeees?"

It's about Matthew. He's OK, but he was arrested in Houston last night and was taken into custody. He will be arraigned and facing a judge this morning and probably be sent to jail to prevent that he would take off—at least until he's transferred back to Boise, Idaho.

155

"How about . . .?"

Nicolas escaped. That's a long story for another time. Both of his bodyguards were shot during some tumultuous action. The Bruce-guy who hunted you in Idaho, was killed. The other is in the care of St. Joseph's hospital here in Houston, seriously wounded.

"When are you coming back?"

Probably tonight but no later than tomorrow. Hannah surprised Patrick by not asking for any details about Matthew and not expressing any emotion. *I have to request something,* Patrick added.

"OK."

Do not talk to anyone in the Gooding Order about this until I'm back and am with you. That includes Isaiah. The only exception is Katie, of course. But no one else. That's important.

"I understand."

They hung up.

Isaiah pretended to not having heard the conversation. He was dying to know who had called and what exactly was said, but he had a pretty good inkling about what it might be. He left the office shortly after.

Hannah went home as well, and as soon as she was inside, she called Katie.

"Patrick just called. The police have busted the biofuel scam. There was a shooting. One person is dead, another is in the hospital. Matthew is OK but is in police custody."

"When is Patrick coming home?"

Hannah smiled and relayed what Patrick had said. She noticed the sigh in the other end. "Do you want to go out for dinner tonight?" Hannah asked.

"I'd love to. Sounds like we can go anywhere we want," Katie said and they decided on time and place.

"See you later," they said in unison.

CHAPTER FORTY-TWO

AT THE FRONT DESK OF St. Joseph Medical Center, Jasmine got direction to the Intensive Care room where Stan had been transferred overnight.

Outside the room, the nurse informed Jasmine that Stan's condition after abdominal surgery was serious but stable. "His liver and part of the transverse colon had been lacerated and he lost a lot of blood. Fortunately, his spine had not been damaged." The nurse urged Jasmine to make the visit brief as Stan was too weak to stand extensive questioning.

Stan didn't hear Jasmine opening the door and slowly approaching the bed. Except for his slow, labored, and oxygen-assisted breathing and the incessant beeping of instruments that surrounded him, it was dead silent in the room. Jasmine could even hear the drops of medicine going into the fluid bottle that was connected to his body.

He looked peaceful. The long, blonde hair was a bit matted and the color was gone from his tan, still ruggedly handsome face.

While he slept, Jasmine strategized how she could maximize the value of this man in the next coming days or perhaps weeks. After about ten-fifteen minutes, Stan stirred. He tried to turn but realized he couldn't and fell back with a moan. He blinked several times.

"You? . . . Again?" he whispered when he opened his eyes and tried to smile. The light from the window behind Jasmine blinded Stan. Jasmine got up and closed the blinds.

"Thank . . . you."

"How do you feel?" Jasmine asked gently but regretted the stupid question. 'Duh! How does one feel after being shot and having major surgery? Hot? Probably not.'

"Rotten . . . I, eh, wish . . . you had killed me." He tried to smile again.

"Maybe next time," Jasmine said and reached forward and squeezed his hand. "Do you remember what happened yesterday?"

"Sure . . . like it was . . . yesterday!"

Jasmine was amazed by his will power to display a sense of humor. He had all the reasons in the world not to speak. Stan pushed the nurse call-button, and when she came in he asked her to raise him up. She gently helped him up, "but it can only be fifteen degrees," she added before she left. Stan nodded.

"I was going to ask you some question, but I'll limit it to one for today and come back again tomorrow. During the chaos yesterday, when you were lying on the floor, you looked at me and said, 'I'm sorry.' What did you mean? If you even remember it?"

He took a deep breath and started slowly. "Oh yes. I do . . . I was so sure I was going to die, and . . . I wanted to say . . . that I . . . was so sorry for what . . . happened on *Sirius 2*. I was an asshole and lost my senses." He took a deep breath. "Although we both . . . played the game we had to play . . . you didn't deserve that."

Jasmine was stunned. Her eyes moistened for a moment. 'In the moment of possibly dying, he was thinking about *me*?' She realized that despite his roughness on the boat, he was not the type of bodyguard like Bruce, a true fixer and a brutal one if need be. Stan was a 'true bodyguard,' hired to *protect* Nicolas and his property—not to attack anyone. She took his hand.

"Thank you, Stan. I really mean it."

"I've been thinking . . ." Stan grimaced when pain shot through his body.

"Yes?"

"Maybe . . . later," he whispered.

"You know what? I'll be back tomorrow morning. Ten o'clock seems like the time we always get together," she said with a big smile, "and if you have the energy, there's something I'd like to discuss, too."

"Thanks . . . Jasmine." He squeezed her hand and held it for a moment.

#

Linda, Captain Hales, and Jasmine had an hour-long meeting about how to find and capture Nicolas. The nascent connection Stan and Jasmine had made under these extraordinary conditions made her bold and confident, so Jasmine outlined an idea she had conceived while driving back from the hospital. It was received as "brilliant," and "if you think it has a chance," they both said, "let's go for it. We don't know where to look for him, so it's a better strategy than any other one we have at the moment.

"When we'rre back in Salt Lake City," Linda continued, "I'll focus on how I can integrate your plan into how I think we can get close to Nicolas. I think the two together can produce results in a short amount of time. I want to meet for fifteen minutes every morning.

"Good luck tomorrow," Linda said in closing the meeting.

#

The next day at 10 a.m., Jasmine entered St. Joseph's. She knew the way to the Intensive Care Unit and went straight to Stan's room.

Stan sat up—at a 15 degrees angle as the nurse had commanded—when Jasmine entered. He had a little color in his cheeks and the oxygen tube had been removed from his nose. She quietly approached the bed and stood at the side for a moment, holding his hand before she sat down.

"Good morning," she said. "How are you today?"

"Better, thanks. I guess it's helpful to be in good shape. And to have a good night's sleep—with a lot of help from the meds I got. The doctor thinks, by the way, I may only need minor follow-up surgery. A 'patchwork' he called it."

"That's wonderful."

"Yeah. I think I was lucky."

Stan took a deep breath and said, "When you left yesterday, I said I'd been thinking. I do that occasionally and only with great caution." His smile was strained but charming. "I want to apologize for what happened on *Sirius 2*. I was a jerk and . . ."

"Yes, you were, but you *did* say that yesterday." Of course he forgot that under the cloud of drugs. "So let's put that behind us." She smiled at him.

"Oh, good. Well, in that case you can leave." He controlled his laughter when he watched Jasmine sitting with her mouth open. "I mean . . . " He moaned. "What I really wanted to say . . . before I ran out of breath, was . . . He paused again.

"I . . . eh, wish there would be an opportunity for a second chance to . . . prove I'm actually a gentleman. You have no reason to trust me and no reason to say 'yes,' but I wanted to say it anyway." He closed his eyes and rested for a moment. Jasmine could tell how important it had been for Stan to say that and how much energy he had to put into it. She almost choked as she took his hand.

"You know what, Stan? You're a good man. Can I ask how you got involved in the business of Nicolas?" Jasmine's attitude invigorated him.

"Sure. Simple enough. I needed a job. I was tired of corporate security work. It doesn't pay all that well and has odd hours. Even though I don't have a family, it's an awkward lifestyle. When I heard about Sirius wanting two-to-three bodyguards, I met with Nicolas. The pay was out of this world. I thought he joked, but he was serious. Maybe that's why he calls everything around him 'Sirius.' Sorry, that was lame." Jasmine shook her head, smiling. 'Nothing shallow about that man,' she thought.

"I mean, a six figure income for protecting a man sounded like something I could do. Although it *can* be around the clock, it's typically day time hours." He paused while thinking what else there was so say about the job. Jasmine let him take his time. She had a feeling that what was coming next was exactly what she wanted to hear.

"As far as I was concerned, I was never a hit man. And Nicolas knew that. That's why I spent a lot of time on the yacht—protecting *property*. Some of the other guys and one girl have a different attitude about the job. Bruce being one. Kenny another." Having met the 'one girl,' Jasmine thought is was misplaced to call Jane a girl, but that was the term for a woman in that business, she reckoned.

"May I interrupt? I should tell you that Bruce died in the conference room during the chaos."

"Oh!" He reflected upon the news for a moment. "It's always tragic, but . . ." He didn't finish the sentence because he wanted to get back to the point. "But thanks for telling me.

"So, about attitudes. To me it was all about protecting Nicolas. I typically do not carry a weapon as you perhaps noticed when you were on the yacht *and* at the meeting the other day. That was supposed to be a business meeting with a person Nicolas had met before, so why carry a gun? I had no inkling it was a sting operation. And I had no inkling of *why* it was set up. To me, it was just another meeting. What I heard in the first fifteen minutes of the meeting totally blew me away. I do *not* want to be associated with any of that again in the future.

"Anyway . . . I'm glad I wasn't armed at the meeting. I might have shot you," Stan said. When he chuckled he placed his arm over his belly because of the pain. Jasmine laughed, too, and realized she had held his hand while he talked. She let go of it.

"Well, I'm glad, too. And I'm glad I shot Bruce and not you. You *are* a gentleman. I, eh . . . should give you an answer to your question. Yes, I'll give you a chance to prove you're a gentleman."

"Seriously?" Stan frowned and cocked his head slightly. He was concerned she was posturing or there was a hidden agenda, but Jasmine's eyes didn't lie. "Thank you," he whispered. "But I need to get out of this place first."

"Oh, I thought you might invite me to share a hospital meal with you." Through the pain, Stan laughed heartedly. "Just kidding," Jasmine added, "I'd actually like to be back on *Sirius 2*. We didn't even get to the dessert last time. And I didn't get a chance to finish telling you about the Green Line."

Stan frowned again, puzzled. "Why *Sirius 2*?"

"It could be anywhere, of course, but I have a plan. I have a strong feeling Nicolas will go back there. There are only a few places he can go to . . . if he even can get out of this country, that is. We have taken possession of his airplane sitting here in Houston Airport and of *Sirius* in Santa Monica and *Sirius 2* in Lanarca. But he doesn't know that. So, here's my plan."

'OK. There *is* an agenda,' Stan thought, 'but obviously not 'hidden' since she's going to tell me . . . if what she's going to tell me is correct.' Stan hesitated but decided he shouldn't be concerned about it. He should trust her. "OK," he said, "I'm listening."

As Jasmine went through the steps she had laid out in her mind, Stan shook his head ever so slightly. 'She's one amazing woman,' he thought. 'I can do that. I want to do that.' He nodded several times.

"I'll be back again late this afternoon with a few follow-up things. "Maybe we *can* have a hospital meal together tonight." She got up and kissed Stan on the forehead and left. When she turned around on the way out, she saw Stan lie back with his eyes closed and a smile on his face.

That afternoon, Jasmine brought an IMSI along to Stan's room. She had informed the nurse station about it when she left earlier in the day and the hospital had approved placing it in whatever room Stan would be in over the next period of time. After some small talk, Jasmine explained to Stan how the IMSI worked.

"Oh my God. That's how you obtained all this information that led to the sting? All the way from the conversation I had with the bank director in Nicosia? To the trapping of Bruce and Kenny and Jane. Oh my God." Stan was overwhelmed by the sophistication and the simplicity at the same time. Jasmine nodded quietly.

"OK, back to this IMSI" Stan said. "So, you will be spying on me and recording my calls for as long as I'm here?" he asked jokingly.

"On your normal phone, yes absolutely, so talk nicely to you mom. But don't say to *anyone* that the conversations are being recorded," she emphasized. Stan nodded. "And I want you to have a good number of the calls with Nicolas from that phone. Convince him you are his loyal bodyguard, even trash talk me and Eddie and Linda Barnes if you wish. Nicolas will like to hear that, I'm sure.

"I'll have to go back to Salt Lake City with my boss tonight, but I will call you every day to hear how you're doing and to know when you're being released. Call me as often as you wish. For *any* conversation between the two of us, use *only* this burner phone," she emphasized as she handed a cell phone to Stan. "I'm the only one who has *your* number, so you know it's me when it rings." Stan nodded.

When Jasmine got up, Stan held her back. "One more thing," he said. "You mentioned *Sirius 2*. I agree Nicolas may try to go there, but he knows you have been onboard *Sirius 2* and *may* even guard it, so he will more likely go to *Sirius 3* in Agrigento on Sicily, Italy. Only a few people know about that one."

"Sicily? Oh, my goodness. I'm glad you mentioned that. You have already improved my plan. Thanks a million."

CHAPTER FORTY-THREE

NICOLAS AND STAN TALKED FOR only a few minutes about the meeting in Houston. Nicolas was not one bit apologetic about any of it. As a matter of fact, it sounded to Stan like Nicolas was mad at Linda and her team for "cheating" and having created "a fake Demirci "as the trap. Stan wholeheartedly agreed.

"How on Earth are they capable of doing that?" Nicolas asked. It was a rhetorical question but Stan answered anyway, "I have no clue, but I guess the police and FBI or whomever was involved have high tech stuff that can trace everything. Probably even illegal," he added with a chuckle.

"Now, tell me, how are you doing?"

"I'm OK. They could sew me together. It hurts like Hell but I'm improving every day. And they only need to do a little patchwork in a second surgery a few months from now to fix me up completely."

"God, I'm glad to hear that," Nicolas said. *"How long are they going to keep you there?"*

"Probably a week or two. They don't want to put me on an airplane to go home, thank goodness. If I lived here in Houston, they'd send me home in a day or two. So, yeah, one-to-two weeks, I guess, but with your permission, I'd like to take a week off, may a little more, afterwards to go and see my mom in Portland before I come back to Santa Monica and become active again."

"Sure you want to do this kind of work?"

"Heck yeah! That's the only kind of work I know. Besides taking care of *Sirius 2* or any of the yachts is what I love."

"Well, I'd love to have you back."

"I hoped you would say that, boss. So, where are you now?" Stan asked in a voice as neutral as if he'd ask for the time of the day.

"I can't tell you."

"Because you don't . . ."

"Because it's not good for you to know."

"OK, boss, whatever you think is best. I hope to see you soon. And thanks for wanting me back. I was a little concerned . . . I'll call regularly and let you know how things progress."

"Please do."

They hung up.

#

"That was a very good first call," Jasmine said when she called Stan on the burner phone. *"How are you* truly *doing?"*

"Thanks, new boss. I'm doing better. Will start physical therapy later this week, by the way. It'll hurt, but they say I will heal faster if I get out of bed as soon as I can."

#

The following day, Jasmine called Stan on his burner.

"We have just intercepted a text from Nicolas that he wants *Sirius 3* to be prepared for a trip to Pantelleria Island in the Mediterranean Sea. I'm so glad you told me that yesterday. My focus was entirely on Lanarca. I have to look that place up, by the way.

"I need the phone number of the person in charge on *Sirius 3*."

"I'll text you when we hang up," Stan said.

An hour later, she and Eddie had the captain's phone number and Kram had gotten inside it. Jasmine sat in Eddie's office in Salt Lake City when the text message from Nicolas appeared on their screen:

> *I will fly in to Palermo Friday p.m. and drive to Agrigento the same night. Will stay overnight on Sirius 3 and sail out to Pantelleria Island sometime Saturday morning or Noon. See you Friday.*
> *Nicolas d'*

A few moments later, Jasmine read the response from the captain:

> *Roger that, Sir.*
> *I'm glad to hear that. Everything will be ready for you.*
> *Ciao - Ferdinando*

CHAPTER FORTY-FOUR

"TIME TO PACK," LINDA SAID at the Monday morning meeting.

"We should be on Sicily the day before Nicolas arrives. I know nothing about Pantelleria Island other than what I see on my laptop right now. Lovely place, but small. There's nothing there other than a national park and a tiny resort, Le Lanterne. That is a great place to hide, or so it seems, but you probably also stand out very easily."

"My guess is," Jasmine said, "that Nicolas will try to disappear from there into Tunisia—to the city of Tunis most likely. I'd like to have some Interpol people in the region and maybe one or two from FBI. We cannot let him slip in to Tunis, if that's where he's going. There are too many places we cannot cover."

"Great analysis, Jasmine," Linda said. "Thank you."

"We owe great thanks to Stan, though. Had it not been for him, we would sit on Cyprus on Friday." Jasmine said. Linda hid her smile. 'She more than likes him,' Linda thought and nodded.

"Eddie, can we get Kram to find out which plane Nicolas is on?" Linda asked. "We need to verify his traveling plan . . . if he sticks to the plan we think he has?"

"I'll put him on it right away."

Twenty minutes later, Eddie had Kram's answer.

"Nicolas is booked for arriving in Palermo at 6:55 p.m. on Friday, flying in from Rome where he has been since two days after we all were in Houston. He must have moved around using cash all the way, but two days ago, he paid an airbnb with PayPal linked to his credit card. Unwise, clearly, but they often don't take cash."

"Wow," Linda said, "So he slipped out of the U.S. under our watch. Well, it *is* a big area to cover.

"Anyway, Jasmine and Eddie, we'll go to Palermo on Thursday and fly to Pantelleria the next morning. That gives us Friday to get ready for Nicolas's arrival the next day. I'll call FBI in Rome and ask them to put Sergio on a plane to Pantelleria so he's there when *we* arrive. We need to have a native Italian renting a boat in the local marina the day before Nicolas arrives. That gives us flexibility if Nicolas changes his plans."

"Also, have Kram confirm that Nicolas arrives in Palermo and that *Sirius 3* does leave Agrigento Saturday morning," Jasmine said.

"And if you can, have an FBI drone check that *Sirius 3* sails towards Pantelleria and not somewhere else—without making contact with the yacht, of course."

#

Pantelleria was a lovely spot. The harbor was filled with impressive yachts, 'hiding from prying eyes?' Linda thought.

Her group spent all Friday morning together with Sergio getting familiar with the place. Sergio had asked the harbor master for the only large mooring spot left. "Mi dispiace," he said. "It's reserved for an American who comes Saturday afternoon or evening. But you can have the smaller one right across from *Sirius 3*, that's her name, by the way," said the harbor master. Sergio chose that spot and joked about having *Il Tramonto*—meaning The Sunset—across from *Sirius*, the Morning Star.

After going through all the logistics and possible scenarios about what might happen, the group had lunch and spent the rest of the day visiting the newly founded National Park. Despite its small size— about 25 square miles—'it covers 80% of the volcanic island,' the entry sign informed visitors. A charming, rocky place, they all thought. "I think I could settle here," Jasmine said. "Who knows, they might need a Chief of Police," she joked.

They had a quiet dinner at the harbor café. They all had the unknowns of the next day on their minds. Although they had planned for all possibilities, "commando raids" of this nature are always guesswork," Linda warned. "Improvisation is critical. As is communication. And one hundred percent trust in one another."

Saturday came . . . and Saturday went.

In the evening, Sergio checked with the harbor master if *Sirius 3* was coming or not, gently using the excuse that if not, he certainly would like the larger moor for *Il Tramonto*. The harbor master assured Sergio that *Sirius 3* would be coming. "They have called and informed us about a technical delay."

Linda decided to stay up all night to see what might happen.

Around 2 a.m. Sunday morning, the broad catamaran-structured *Sirius 3* slowly pulled into Pantelleria harbor. Linda decided not to go to bed but instead watch for any activity on deck.

She thought she saw a glimpse of Nicolas but without a binocular she couldn't be sure.

The only other activity that early morning was a small motor boat arriving and anchoring up in front of *Sirius 3*.

CHAPTER FORTY-FIVE

AROUND 9 A.M. SUNDAY MORNING, Sergio was out walking on the piers of the harbor. The sky was already *azzuri*, as the local would call it, and cloudless. The Sun hadn't yet gained the power that would force people indoors in the afternoons, and the ocean breeze was pleasant. A perfect day to be on the water or in the parks. Several kinds of gulls, plovers, terns and kingfishers were enjoying the serene morning, too, perched on poles, masts, and powerlines and filling the air with their songs and chirps. Segio wondered why there weren't more people out.

Everything on and around *Sirius 3* was quiet, but when Sergio walked by it a third time, he saw the captain on the bridge. Sergio did a sailor's greeting with two fingers tapping his right temple, which the captain reciprocated.

Sergio went to the harbor café and sat down outside at a small, round marble table and ordered an espresso and a ciabatta when the waiter tended to him. Sergio was reading the Sicilian morning newspaper when captain Ferdinando walked in.

"Ciao," the two men said in a greeting and when Sergio nodded his accept of Ferdinando's gesture towards the chair at the table, Ferdinando sat down. He, too, ordered an espresso and a ciabatta. The two captains chatted about their trip to Pantelleria, a first for both of them. Ferdinando told Sergio that a problem with a bilge pump shortly after leaving Agrigento had forced them to return to port to fix it. "Otherwise, it was pretty smooth sailing," he said.

Sergio talked about the British tourists on his yacht who had visited Tunisia for a couple of days and now wanted to cruise the Mediterranean for a week or so. Ferdinando's passengers were New Yorkers who would be touring the island and spend time hiking before heading off to Malta in a few days.

"Aren't you joining them? On the hike, I mean," asked Sergio.

"Nah, I'll stay onboard and relax. I'm running around enough as it is. Maybe you want to come over when they are out this afternoon. For a glass of wine."

"Oh, that would be great," Sergio said. "Thank you. What time?"

"Say, is three o'clock good?"

"Perfetto. Gracias."

They finished their coffee and ciabatta, got up, and nodded goodbye. Ferdinando went to the long pier and Sergio went around to the other side and boarded *Il Tramonto*.

Over lunch, Sergio briefed the group on the conversation with Ferdinando. "He lied as much as I did. Maybe that's an instruction from Nicolas not to give away any information that may reveal who the passengers are, or how many, so we must tread very carefully. "

After a long conversation, they had their plans ready.

#

Linda, Jasmine and Eddie sat on a bench on the pier where *Sirius 3* was anchored, taking in the view of the marina and enjoying the afternoon. They watched Sergio board the yacht at precisely 3 p.m.. Once onboard and greeted by Ferdinando, Sergio was shown around on the yacht. It was huge and impressive. There was a machine engineer onboard, a chef, and a purser or household manager. They greeted Sergio cordially and returned to their duties when Sergio was shown the belowdeck facilities.

While they were downstairs, Linda, Jasmine, and Eddie quietly walked onboard and hid along the port side near the stern and out of view from the captain's bridge. When Ferdinando and Sergio came up from below, they went to the sun deck on the stern. Immediately after sitting down, drinks and snacks were served.

Linda moved soundlessly out from the hiding spot and stood right behind Ferdinando before he noticed something was wrong. He spun around and gasped when he looked into the barrel of Linda's Glock 19 handgun.

"What the Hell is . . .?" He raised his hands in a defensive position.

"Listen carefully. If you follow my instructions, promptly and to the T, you're safe. We're not here for you."

"We?"

"My partners are with me but you won't see them. And you don't need to know who I am. Now get up."

Ferdinando hesitated.

"Don't make me repeat myself." She motioned with the gun that she wanted Ferdinando to get up.

"Hand me your phone." With that in her pocket, Linda said, "Take me to the intercom center." Once in front of it on the captain's bridge, Linda said, "Disable all communication on the yacht." When Ferdinando hesitated, Linda raised the gun and turned the safety off. The click got Ferdinando's attention and he flipped all communication switches off.

"Good. Now, walk downstairs. Slowly." On the way across the deck, Eddie joined them.

Ferdinando looked at him with a fury stare but walked to the stairs leading belowdeck.

"Where to?" he asked.

"The sleeping quarters."

When they got there, Linda ordered Ferdinando into the main sleeping salon. "Sam will stay outside the door, right here. He's armed, so don't try anything." Eddie showed Ferdinando his Sig SAUER gun. "Thanks, Sam," Linda said and Eddie closed the door. Linda whispered, "I need him up on the deck when Nicolas comes, so he doesn't sense anything is wrong. I'll text you to that effect."

Linda and Jasmine familiarized themselves with the layout of the sun deck. "We'll sit here until Nicolas comes. Oh, dang! I forgot to ask how many people are in the hiking group." She texted Eddie who got the answer from Ferdinando. *Just one other, he says.*

"If that's true, two people will be here. Let's be prepared for the fact that there might be more."

Fifteen minutes later, Linda spotted Nicolas and a woman coming out of the dock master's office and heading towards *Sirius 3*. She texted Eddie.

Send Ferdinando up on the sun deck. Two minutes later, Ferdinando sat next to Linda, Jasmine and Sergio. Ferdinando looked at Sergio with a hateful expression.

"Don't look at me that way," Sergio said, "I've no idea what's going on." Ferdinando didn't buy that.

Nicolas and the woman—'a girl, rather,' Linda thought as she saw her closer up—walked hand in hand until they reached *Sirius 3*. Nicolas looked around before he stepped onto the walkway to the yacht, then continued up to the sundeck with the girl. He spotted the three guests sitting with their drinks, facing away from him.

"Who's here?" he grunted at Ferdinando.

"Sailors from the boat over there," Ferdinando pointed to the other pier.

"What are they doing here?"

"They, eh . . ."

"We just stopped by to see you, Nicolas," Linda said as she and Jasmine got up with guns pointed at him. Nicolas stared at them, dumbfounded and lost for words.

"We didn't finish our business in Houston," Linda said, "so we thought we'd stop by. Such a lovely afternoon, isn't it? Please," Linda said, gesturing to Nicolas—ignoring the girl— to sit next to her. "Have a drink with us."

Nicolas didn't move.

CHAPTER FORTY-SIX

IN ONE QUICK MOTION, NICOLAS pulled the girl in front of himself as a shield. She screamed. "What are you doing? What's going . . .?"

"Quiet," Nicolas barked at her.

Wide eyed and terrified, the girl kicked wildly and screamed for help—to no avail. Nicolas kept her in an iron grip. He had never expected he would need a gun in his own 'home' in such a tiny, far away corner of the world, so he didn't carry one at this time. There was one on the bridge, of course, but he couldn't get to it under the circumstances.

He pressed his index finger into the area between the girl's shoulderblades, pretending it was a handgun. The girl struggled but Nicolas tightened the iron grip, preventing her from slipping away.

He knew he was a sitting duck and that there was only one way out of the situation. He slowly backed away from Linda and Jasmine, who approached him equally slowly and six feet apart, so if Nicolas indeed had a gun, he could only shoot at one of them before the other would shoot back. Nicolas kept backing up and Linda and Jasmine kept following. When he was close enough to the stairs leading belowdeck, Nicolas spun around, leaving the girl to block the view and preventing Linda and Jasmine from shooting. The girl fell to her knees and rolled into a ball as small as she could make it.

"Don't shoot, don't shoot," she cried out.

"Don't worry. You're safe," Linda said. "Go over to the table and sit down." The girl got up and tip-toed to the table, still terrified and bewildered.

Nicolas stormed downstairs and came face to face with Eddie.

Nicolas was shocked and confused, thinking he saw Demirci. In a flash, though, he realized it was the FBI agent.

Nicolas had the advantage of coming from above and he jumped from the stairs onto Eddie's chest before Eddie could shoot. Eddie stumbled backwards and knocked his head on the floor, momentarily making him defenseless. Without a gun and not being able to eliminate Eddie, Nicolas was entirely focused on escaping and ran around the sleeping quarters toward the lower port on the yacht where two jet skis were parked. Just as Nicolas jump-started a big Yamaha, Eddie had gotten up and came around the master bedroom, aiming his gun at the jet ski and fired. The gas tank blew up in a ball of fire. Nicolas was knocked off the waterski but managed to throw himself into the water.

Updeck, Jasmine ran to the stern and looked down. She spotted Nicolas but he saw her before she could release a shot. Nicolas disappeared into the dark water and with a few strong strokes he swam in between the two keels of the catamaran where he could breathe. Nicolas could hide there for a few moments, but he knew he would be trapped if he stayed for long. He swam slowly toward the bow of the yacht and peered up. Seeing no one above him, he filled his lungs with one huge gasp of air and swam underwater towards the pier. Old iron steps anchored intermittently along the pier wall led to the top. It was tempting to try to get up, but he couldn't get there unnoticed.

Nicolas had no other option to stay hidden than to aim for a small motorboat 50 yards ahead of *Sirius 3*. He was clinging as closely to the pier wall as he could and was careful not to make ripples in the water that could be seen and would make noise. He wondered if he could do this long enough to reach the boat without being spotted, but it was his best chance. The Sun was getting low over the mountains in the west so the pier and the port side of boats and yachts were in the shade. That added a bit of an extra cover for Nicholas.

Eddie had come up to the sundeck where Jasmine was still scanning the water where Nicolas had disappeared. Linda and Sergio watched over Ferdinando and the girl at the table, keeping them from moving by pointing their guns at them. That allowed Eddie to immediately head for the walkway to the pier, assuming Nicolas would appear somewhere on land. He was followed by Jasmine. They walked ever so slowly along the pier while keeping their eyes peeled on *Sirius 3*.

Nicolas managed to get to the motorboat without Eddie and Jasmine spotting him. After several agonizingly slow minutes, Nicolas made it into the narrow space between the pier wall and the hull of the motor boat where he reached for a large fender. He grabbed the thick rope and slowly pulled himself upwards. When he was far enough up to reach the boat railing, he swung one leg over the edge and landed, clumsily but securely, on the deck. He lifted his head and saw Eddie and Jasmine both looking into the water in front of *Sirius 3*. But not in his direction—yet.

Nicolas snaked his way to the portside of the boat where he rested for a moment. He slipped out of his shoes, trousers, and polo shirt; being half-naked would make him look like a crew member being outside on deck enjoying the afternoon.

Nicolas listenened for any sound coming from anywhere on the boat that would indicate people were onboard. After concluding he was alone, he got up and approached the bridge carefully. It was vacated. He searched the bridge for handguns but didn't find any, went downstairs to the sleeping quarters, rummaged through cabinets and dressers, found a sailor's cap and put it on. He tried the lockers in the hallway. Two were filled with a large collection of fishing gear and, to his delight, in the third there was a 9 mm Smith & Wesson M&P and a box with just 5 bullets left. He grabbed the gun and kept the bullets in his hand. 'That has to do. No room for missing,' he thought.

He left the lights on in the belowdeck rooms to make it look like people were onboard.

Just as he was about to go back up to the bridge, hoping to be able to power up the boat and sail away, he heard footsteps.

He was not alone.

Worse than that . . . he was now trapped belowdeck.

CHAPTER FORTY-SEVEN

THE FOOTSTEPS SOUNDED CLOSER NOW and Nicolas could hear the voices of a man and woman. They could be downstairs in a minute.

He loaded the gun and clicked the safety off. The voices got more distinct. Mid-aged, he assessed. The man was talking but Nicolas didn't understand the words. 'German, perhaps?' he was guessing. They seemed to be chatting very casually, surely not expecting anything to be out of the ordinary. Nicolas moved away from the master bedroom and stood silently in a dark corner of the hallway, suppressing his breath.

A woman came belowdeck and disappeared into the bedroom. Seconds later, a man came and went the same way, closing the door behind him. 'Now, *they* are trapped,' Nicolas thought with a smile. There was no talking in the bedroom and he heard no water running. 'They're probably changing clothes. Good time to surprise them.'

With a forceful shoulder push, Nicolas forced the flimsy door open and took a step inside, gun in hand, standing still, holding his breath. Looking. Listening. Stunned.

There was not a soul in the room.

Nicolas took another step into the room. Other than faint harbor sounds, it was dead silent. The bathroom door was open but there was no one in there either. The bed was a platform bed, so no one could be underneath. 'And why would they?' Nicolas reasoned. There was no other exits and the porthole was too small for a person to slip through. 'And why would they?' he reasoned again.

That raised the alarm.

'Something's awfully wrong with this scenario. Where the . . .?' In a flash Nicolas realized where the couple was, but before he could turn he heard Eddie's voice very close behind him.

"Don't move!" he said threatening. "Don't even think about it. Put your hands on your head." Eddie, who had stepped out from behind the door, pressed his gun in between Nicolas's shoulderblades. With the butt of her gun, Jasmine —who stood shoulder by shoulder with Eddie—aimed her swing at the back of Nicolas's head just as he turned to face them. She missed the precise target and Nicolas stumbled forward, but was not out. Despite the pain, he managed to fire three shots over his shoulder without looking back.

The first two shots missed them but the third hit Jasmine in the chest. Her Kevlar vest saved her but she was knocked backwards towards Eddie. In one motion, he sidestepped Jasmine's body, let her drop to the floor, and fired a single shot from an awkward position. It hit Nicolas in the thigh but he managed to get up on both feet and staggered away, heading upstairs toward the deck.

Eddie threw himself forward and caught Nicolas around the legs just as Nicolas took the first steps upwards. Nicolas fell and landed face down on the steps with a heavy thump. He brought his hand around behind his back and released two wild shots. Both missed their targets. He pulled the trigger again but the gun was empty.

Out of bullets, Nicolas tried to hit Eddie with the butt of the gun, but Eddie covered himself under Nicolas's lower body. Two other shots rang out and Eddie felt the violent spasms under him. Seconds later, Nicolas went limp on the stairs. As Jasmine approached Nicolas and Eddie, she held her gun in front of her in case she needed to fire again. That was not necessary.

Nicolas was lifeless.

Eddie got up.

"That was one heck of a risky shot, Jasmine. You missed me by an inch." There was a trace of anger and disbelief in his voice.

"I was certain of my aim on that distance."

"You're wounded. That's a challenge to any good aim. And it was a moving target."

"I know, but . . ."

"Anyway. Well done, partner. Let's get back up to the group. We need to take a good look at you. And there are a lot of things we need to do tonight and tomorrow."

CHAPTER FORTY-EIGHT

EPILOGUE

MATTHEW WAS TRANSFERRED TO BOISE state prison two weeks after the arrest in Houston. He had not spoken a word to Hannah or his other wives, to Esaiah, to a lawyer, or to anyone else. He had been informed that Nicolas had been killed during a raid on a small island in the Mediterranean Sea. That didn't seem to leave any impression on him but he wondered briefly how Nicolas had managed to get all the way to Europe.

But mostly, Matthew pondered incoherently how the whole network, the whole world had suddenly collapsed around him—despite Nicolas's repeated assurances that it wouldn't. He was utterly bewildered by how the authorities had been able to stage the sting operation in Houston, and there seemed to be no connections between the events he had experienced over the last several years and everything he heard at the meeting. He felt like he was isolated in a parallel universe.

He sat like a mannequin that had been thrown to the side after having served its purpose. He moved as little as possible and acted like a heavily drugged person.

Hannah debated with herself whether to go and see Matthew in jail, but she eventually gave in and drove to Boise. She hadn't seen or heard anything from Esaiah since he left the office on the day Patrick called from Houston, so she didn't know if the two brothers had had any contact since then.

Matthew already sat on the other side of the glass wall, when the prison guard led Hannah into the visitor's room for a metered 30 min conversation.

He was almost unregnizeable in the dark-blue jail jumpsuit. He was pale, his eyes were extinct of any life, and his unkempt hair made him look like a homeless man on the streets. He was cleanly shaved, though. Hannah was shocked, but she was even more shocked that meeting her husband in this condition and under such circumstances had no impact on her. She never thought of herself as an uncaring person, but something inside had died.

"I don't know what to say," Matthew started feebly.

"You don't have to say anything. I came to say goodbye."

"What? What d'you mean?"

"It means you will not see me again."

"But Hannah! . . ." Utter disbelief penetrated his words. He took a deep breath and struggled with controlling his emotions. "But I need you." His eye were begging for mercy. "More than ever."

"You didn't need me for 15 years. You don't need me now. You need God's help. If you have any faith left in you, pray for help."

Matthew put his elbows on the small ledge in front of the glass wall, bent over, and covered his face with his hands. When he looked up, he whispered, "I'm . . . so awfully . . . sorry."

"Me too. Seriously. I'm sad we had to go through this ordeal to get to this point. But here we are."

"Can't we . . ."

"Matthew! Listen to me. There's no 'we' in our future. You have other wives, and kids, too, remember? You don't need *me*."

They sat in silence for some time, not knowing what else to say. Hannah wondered if he understood her words.

"What are you going to do now?" Matthew finally asked.

"I'll move to Idaho Falls. I have two friends there. I'll find a place of my own. There will be enough money from selling the house to sustain me for a long time. I'll be fine."

"You'll sell the house? But . . . what about the Order? Are you . . ."

"I don't need the house. And neither do you—for another ten to twenty years. About the Order? Remember when we talked about Katie running away? You asked me if I thought 'being outside the Order was freedom.' Those were actually Katie's exact words, not mine . . . but you know what? I've learned she was right. I'm free now to shape my own life. For the first time in my life."

They sat in silence until the buzzer went off and the prison guard said, "It's time."

Hannah got up.

"Good luck," she said.

Matthew didn't look up and didn't respond.

She stood for a moment and looked for the last time on a man she had known since early childhood, who came out of nothing and ended up having more than anyone could ever imagine. Unfortunately, plenty was never enough for him—and he lost it all. Although their marriage was not one based on love, she did care for him. He had many good qualities, she admitted. He was brilliant in so many ways, he worked hard. And she knew he in his own strange way cared for her, too.

'But he was . . .' She didn't quite know how best to describe him—and let it go. As she left, she was at peace with herself for being honest when she had said she was sorry.

Sorry and deeply saddened, too.

#

The *Peregrine* group met in Linda's conference room in the Salt Lake City field office.

Eddie and Jasmine had recovered from their "scratches" as they called their injuries from the Mediterranean excursion. Patrick was present as well, although he had not participated in the operation on Pantelleria, and so were Katie and Hannah.

"Well, that was a dramatic conclusion of a very complex and complicated case," Linda said. "I don't remember having one that was so unique in so many respects. And I've been at it for the better part of forty years. And I doubt if FBI have ever worked with two such unlikely moles as Katie and Hannah. And we have worked with many.

"We've attracted a lot of attention in FBI in Washington because of the sophisticated technology and methodology we used, the planning, and the execution by everyone involved. I've been asked to convey to all of you that there will be promotions coming to the FBI'ers in due time. As much as would like to, I can't help you in that regard, Patrick," Linda added with a smile, facing him. "That will be a matter for the police department in Idaho, but I'm sure they recognize your contribution to solving this entire case.

"And I have some good news to share. You may not have paid attention to this, but because of the magnitude of the case, FBI had—eagerly nudged by IRS, I should add—offered up significant rewards for outside individuals who substantially helped the case. Therefore, there will be fifty thousand dollars to each of Katie, Hannah, and Kram."

"Oh, my God," the two women said in unison, looking at one another. "That's unbelievable."

"Yes," Linda said. "We solved a very large financial crime case in addition to two murder cases, and we have the perpetrators in jail. Eddie, you will have to inform Kram about this and ask him how we can facilitate the payment to him shortly."

"I'll be more than happy to do so," Eddie said. "Any information on what's going to happen with Matthew and Isaiah?" Eddie asked.

"It's too early to say, but as we all know, Matthew was taken to the state jail in Idaho a week or so after the meeting in Houston where he had pleaded non-guilty in court and insisted on bail for going free. The judge dismissed that, of course. He's awaiting a sentence, probably in the 20-years range. I'm awfully sorry, Hannah."

"Don't be," Hannah said. "It's not going to be much of an issue for me. Although I was deeply saddened by all this, I was not happy in that relationship. And I don't want to live in the house Matthew bought some years ago, so I'll move to Idaho Falls. When Bruce Hawkeye was trying to find me, I stayed with Patrick and Katie. I like the city."

"You live with . . .?" Linda looked at Patrick. "Oh, I'm sorry, that's none of my business. I appolo . . ."

"Not to worry. She was a target, so she was in 'protective custody'. . . at my place," Patrick said and couldn't help laughing about the choice of words. "But we are actually thinking about moving together." He smiled shyly. Katie blushed. "Now that the mole has come out of hiding," he added.

"Well, good for both of you. Well . . . Oh, yes, that brings me to Jane Easton in Atlanta." Linda nodded in the direction of Jasmine and said, "You deserve an Oscar for best acting on that whole trip. Her murder trial is still pending, by the way. Same with Kenny.

"And that leaves Rita and Isaiah. Rita's role was as a board member. Although she sat in on meetings and knew what was going on, her role was passive, and given her, shall we call it "subordinate status" of being a woman in the Order, she didn't have much of a choice. She has been arrested, of course, but her sentence will be mild; that's my guess.

"About Isaiah. He's definitely guilty as a participant in criminal, fraudulent transactions and in making false reporting to IRS and EPA.

He may get away with some leniency because according to what we hear from Hannah and Katie, he was increasingly concerned about the transactions and believed the business was out of control. He wanted to slow it down or stop entirely. That speaks in his favor as does the fact that being a member of the Order and being a younger brother, he had no choice other than doing what he was told to do."

"Where *is* he, by the way?" Eddie asked.

"He left his office right after I got Patrick's phone call from Houston," Hannah said. "He didn't know the precise content of the conversation, of course, but I'm sure he had a pretty good feel for it. I left shortly after he did, by the way, and I haven't seen or heard from him since. No one in the Order has—from the little I know, I should say. He's not in his house where he lives by himself. I know that, too, because I stopped by there before I went to Boise to see Matthew the other day. I asked Isaiah's neighbors, but they haven't seen him either.

"Mind you, he's a knowledgeable, very skillful woodsman, so he can disappear in Idaho—or anywhere for that matter—and be perfectly safe for a long, long time. Alone undoubtedly, but safe. I guess I'd call him 'an escapee,'" Hannah added with a smile.

"Well, that's for the police in Idaho to deal with—good luck with that, Patrick. I think . . ."

"May I?" Hannah raised her hand. "Just a consideration?"

Linda nodded.

"I'm not in a position to give either one of you advice, but I know Isaiah very well. He once said to me, that he didn't feel like an equal partner with Matthew, who had only his own good fortune in mind." She hesitated. "So, eh, for what it's worth, Patrick, I would let him be . . . wherever he is."

Patrick hesitated before he said, "I'll have to think about that, Hannah, but thank you for pointing that out."

"Anyway," Linda said, "what I was going to say was: I think we have done enough on this case. There's a lot of clean-up work to do for a lot of people. IRS will start collecting huge fortunes in yachts, houses, land in Romania and Turkey, living residences and Lamborghinis in California and elsewhere, and probably a lot more we don't even know about yet."

"Just leave one of the *Sirius* yachts to Stan," Jasmine added quietly. "They are his life." It was said for fun and she knew it was wishful thinking.

"Oh, on that note," Linda said, ignoring the comment, "I have accepted Jasmine's request for one month sabbatical." She looked at Jasmine and added. "You want to travel to the Mediterranean area, if I understand it correctly? Maybe do a little snorkling and boating?" Linda said with a smile.

Jasmine covered her eyes, shyly, for a second and nodded. The blushing in her cheeks showed under her dark skin tone.

Jokingly, she said with a smile, "Or, like I said before, maybe I'll apply for a job as Chief of Police on Pantelleria—if that even exists."

Linda shook her head, smiling.

'Kids, nowadays,' she thought.

OTHER BOOKS BY TORBEN RIISE

TORBEN RIISE has published the following books in paperback, hard cover, and/or as eBooks. They are available in the U.S., Canada, Europe, Mexico, Brazil, Japan, Australia, and India:

FICTION:
- The Rock & The Pebble, 2021
- The Candidate, 2020
- SNIPS, 2019
- Conversations Across Millennium, 2019
- The Eyes of The Sphinx, 2007
- Emily & The Ransom, 2002
- Emily & The Arbic Letter, 2001

NON-FICTION:
- Handbook For Pre-teens Girls, 2023
  (co-written with Emily Kay Wekulo)
- The Latest on Dementia (DK version)
  on schedule to be published 2023
- Dementia Handbook, Eng. Version 2021
- Demens Håndbogen, DK version 2020
- Ordinary People, Extraordinary Experiences, 2018

These books are available in all major book stores, on Amazon, and from the author's website at https://torbenriise.com/books. See also the Author's Page on http://www.amazon.com/author/torbenriise

You can contact Torben Riise on exec.kaizen@gmail.com. He welcomes questions and comments about his books.

Made in the USA
Las Vegas, NV
27 November 2024

12627484R00105